Th
TH ... CT

"My name is Jericho Jones and I have a healthy respect for the business I'm in because it's one where you don't get slapped on the hand for making a mistake—you get dead.

My talent—if you can call it that—is in being an adjuster for organized crime . . . making cold bodies out of warm ones within the ranks of the syndicate families across the country. I work only for the country's crime web where there is always a need for an assassin of the freelance type who doesn't care which way his gun is pointed. Having those qualifications earned me the tag of Judas . . ."

Jericho Jones had a job to do—find Cardinalli's daughter. She had been snatched by a couple of goons from a rival mob, and Jericho had to move fast.

But every time he took a step, there was somebody waiting. With a blackjack, or a .38. Somebody in Cardinalli's organization had to be feeding info to the other side.

But *who*? And *why*?

THE CARDINALLI CONTRACT

E. Richard Johnson

PYRAMID BOOKS ▲ NEW YORK

THE CARDINALLI CONTRACT

A PYRAMID BOOK

Produced by Lyle Kenyon Engel

Pyramid edition published February 1975

ISBN 0-515-03584-X

Library of Congress Catalog Card Number: 74-25086

Printed in Canada

Pyramid Books are published by Pyramid Communications, Inc. Its trademarks, consisting of the word "Pyramid" and the portrayal of a pyramid, are registered in the United States Patent Office.

PYRAMID COMMUNICATIONS, INC.
919 Third Avenue, New York, N.Y. 10022

THE CARDINALLI CONTRACT

CHAPTER ONE

You could never tell what a visit to Chicago would get you. At least, you could never guess in advance what you'd get by visiting that part of the city I was in—the section on the north side between Clark and Dearborn Streets. It had more derelicts and punks per square yard than any other slum section in the country.

On a visit down there you could easily get your throat cut or be jack-rolled with no trouble at all, mainly because those happenings were just common vocations around the area. Even the derelicts tied hard knots in their shoelaces to keep their Salvation Army shoes from being stolen while they slept on park benches or in doorways. And too, you could get mugged, mickied, propositioned and laid, and you could buy anything from heroin to a hot mink coat. It was not the sort of place you'd find a glowing write-up about at your local travel agency.

The area's population was a pretty static one. It consisted of derelicts who stayed there for lack of anyplace else and others who were born into the defeat of the area and couldn't get out. There were even a few who didn't want to get out because they were pimps, pushers or whatever made them money. Money is about the only reason that could justify staying in the north side.

I happened to be paying a visit to the area because I'm not exactly the type of person to check into any of America's finest hotels over on the Magnificent Mile and feel comfortable, even when I can afford it, and at present I could. I just happen to feel better when I stay where I'm close to my work and the type of people I'm used to. It could even be that I'm sort of a snob in reverse and don't care to phony my way along with the Who's Who set. I know who I am. The world of dirt, blood and hot lead is mine.

I was bumming around in the process of working my way through the pay I had left from my last job. I had heard a rumor which hinted of a lot of heat in Chicago that had nothing at all to do with the weather. It was the sort of heat which could make me another payday, because a brewing gang war that was going to cause some dead bodies in the morgue meant money to me.

I wasn't looking for work, but I read all the signs in the newspapers, the barroom whispers and the tips that an underworld ear picks up on the streets. That's the way you had to get those facts because you couldn't expect to see an ad in the local newspaper stating "GANG WAR. MEN NEEDED!" Word had reached me on a beach in California, where I'd had my fill of sun and fun and was ready to drift again. It seemed to be opportunity rattling at my door.

They call me Judas.

My talent, if you can call it that, is in being an adjuster for organized crime. In other words, I earn a living within the ranks of syndicate families across the country by making cold bodies out of warm ones. That means I can't be hired by just anyone to arrange an accident for Uncle Smith after he takes out a heavy insurance policy in Black Rock, Iowa or such. I work only for the country's crime web, where there is always a need for an assassin of the free-lance type who doesn't care which way his gun is pointed. The qualifications have earned me the tag of Judas. My real name is Jericho Jones. I have a healthy respect for the business I'm in because it's one where you don't get slapped on the hand for making a mistake—you get dead.

As I said, I'd turned up in Chicago because something big seemed to be brewing in the rackets, and I thought it could be big enough to have a contract in it for me. I was also there to get some local information on what was going on in case of future contract offers. It paid to know exactly who was doing what. There are some jobs that are so rank even I won't touch them. You could call that an advantage of being a free-lance gun. I wanted to look, listen and then decide if there was anyone in the whole blood-smeared mess worth carrying a gun for.

I'd checked into a hotel on Chicago Avenue on Wednesday evening, then begun my looking and listening as I made the rounds of the dimly lit outhouses which serve as bars. Thursday night I went back to do some more of the same without attracting too much attention. That's one quirk of a place like the north side; it doesn't take much to advertise your presence. I didn't have to introduce myself to anyone. All I had to do was be there. The grapevine took care of the rest.

It could be that my brain was overcooked from too much California sun or that I thought the local talent had a hell of a lot more to do than check on strangers. When you get right down to it, maybe I wasn't paying too much attention. It proved to be a mistake on my part.

I was in my third bar of the evening when I wound up with a spiked drink. I went off to sleep with a rapidly fogging mind telling me that I was being helped toward the doors. There didn't seem to be any doubt that someone knew I was in town.

I woke up to a hard biting pain which pounded behind my eyes with every heartbeat, while the rest of me felt limp and dead with the aftereffects of a dose of chloral hydrate. I didn't try to open my eyes or do anything foolish like that. You don't jump up and scream "Who slipped me the micky?" at a time like this even if you could, and I couldn't. In fact, you don't do anything but listen to the darkness around you while you make an attempt to sort things out before letting it show you're awake.

There were smells and sounds around me that told me I was in an apartment. I could hear the distant sound of traffic on the street and smell the odor of a good cigar. As my mind cleared, I sorted out the voices in the room and knew that there were three men attending our little get-together. From the empty feeling under my left arm, I knew that my .38 wasn't there. I spent about five minutes listening to the men make small talk before I decided that they weren't going to say anything of interest until I was awake. I opened my eyes.

The one behind the desk who was smoking the cigar I had smelled pointed it at me and said, "He's awake. Give him a drink, Kincaid."

My throat was raw and cottony. My tongue felt too thick to talk. I squinted the fuzziness away and watched Kincaid with a gut tightening sensation while he busied himself with the drink. As the name and face clicked in my mind, I wasn't exactly happy, and I switched my gaze to the man behind the desk. I said, "You've got an odd way of asking people in for a drink, Cardinalli."

He chewed at his cigar. "You know me?" he asked.

"Joseph Cardinalli," I said, repeating the grapevine whispers. "Top capo to your disciples here in Chicago and number one turd on top of the dung heap that they call rackets. To your people you're an old Sicily capo. To the cops you're a pain in the ass because you're a big fish with a lot of political pull and they can't touch you. From what I hear, you've got a finger in everything that's dirty, or you run the people who do have their fingers in it, and you own a lot of legitimate industries besides."

He remained expressionless. "Go ahead," he said.

I shrugged loosely, not feeling any too happy about getting fed a micky. "That's the word in the street," I went on. "You also own a home in Highland Park and have a yacht on Lake Michigan, besides a summer home. From almost everyone's view, you've got the world by the ass and can afford to drop a few million at any time without being hurt. You donate to all the right charities and hob-nob with the Fairlawn society set." I paused to grin at him. "In between cocktail parties and giving speeches to the Ladies' Aid, or whoever the hell you give speeches to, you manage to control a lot of dirty rackets without getting any grime on your hands. But . . ." I let it hang in the room like a question before I added, "That's the sort of information a man can pick up off the street." I nodded toward Kincaid, who was still building my drink. "I believe about half of what's said. I could add things like you make it a habit to keep lousy company, if Kincaid's an example, and just now you've got an ass full of trouble from a greasy little punk called Victor Luciano who happens to be Sicilian too and who wants a chunk of the racket action."

I squeezed my eyes shut to ease the pounding in my head. I opened them and said, "And that, Cardinalli, is everything in the damn world that I know about you. I'm not even eager to learn any more because racket men ceased to impress me a long time ago."

"Talkative son-of-a-bitch, ain't he?" Kincaid asked as he handed me the drink.

I gave Kincaid my best smile. "Sweetheart, you can

get yourself knocked on your ass without half trying." I told him seriously, "I don't happen to like you, punk."

"Let it drop," Cardinalli said tiredly. He stared at the end of his cigar absently. He was a compactly built man with broad shoulders and graying hair. From what I knew about him, I could guess his age at about sixty, but easy living and good clothes gave him the appearance of a younger man. Only his dark eyes were old when they shifted back to me. "You don't seem too worried about being here," he said.

I searched my pockets for a cigarette. "You've got all the trouble you need with Luciano, and there's no advantage in putting strangers into the river. Besides, I wouldn't have awakened from the micky if you wanted me dead. So it figures that you want something from me."

"Maybe we just want to find out who you're working for," Kincaid said helpfully. "Then maybe it's the river."

"That's not your style, Kincaid. You like your kills knocked out, tied up or with their backs to you." While I said it, I saw his hands tighten. Kincaid was one of those pale, long fingered boys that you expect to find in drag on a fairy farm. I didn't know if he was geared or not, but I did know that he was a sickly, deadly little killer who got his jollies while working on a man. In his case, I knew inflicting pain was the closest thing to a piece of tail he'd ever found.

He watched me with an expression which told me he'd enjoy cutting on me some. Then Cardinalli said, "So maybe you're partly right about things. I'll give you a little more history too, since you like to listen so much. Everything you said, I've got. Add to that a seventeen year old daughter who's good looking and as spoiled as I managed to make her, and you've got a better picture. You've also got the reason why I went through the trouble of bringing you here, Jones."

I raised an eyebrow at that name. He held up my

wallet, then pulled the driver's license out. "Jericho Jones," he said. "Kansas City. Six feet tall, two hundred pounds. Gray-brown hair and gray eyes. All of that boils down to a description of the Judas when we add the .38 you had under your arm." He smiled tightly, like he didn't do it often. "Besides, we have a few boys around who remember you."

"I think you lost me there for a minute," I said. "So let me get it right. I got fed a micky because you've got a seventeen year old daughter. *That's* the reason I'm here?"

He nodded. "That's right."

"Hell, Cardinalli, you don't need me, you need a baby sitter, and I'm afraid I went out of that business a long time ago. I was never in it, in fact."

Cardinalli mashed his cigar angrily in the ashtray. "You can cut the smart talk anytime, Jones. I got you here for a job, and I'm not so damn sure it wasn't a mistake."

"Fine," I said. "You can just call it a mistake. I'll get my hat and go."

"You'll go all right," Kincaid said.

"Shut up," Cardinalli said, like he wasn't too happy with the situation. "Let's get down to business." He opened the desk drawer and produced a framed glossy print which he tossed casually into my lap. His eyes had all the emotion of a cesspool. I knew it was time to stop playing hardass. I picked the photo up and examined the girl staring back at me. At seventeen, she was one hell of a lot of woman. The photo was in color. She had large dark eyes which peered at you from a gentle wave of black hair. Her full lips looked soft over her smile. She was in a two-piece swimsuit that showed all the right curves in the right places, and the ninety percent of her skin that I could see was tanned bronze. Judging from the car she was leaning against, I'd guess her height about five foot three and her weight at a hundred and ten pounds with a good dinner in her. There was nothing at all little girlish in the picture.

"Nice looking kid," I said. "What am I supposed to do? Take on a job of rounding up the guest of honor for a shotgun wedding?"

"I wish it were that simple," Cardinalli sighed. "Her name is Sandy. She's my only child. The way things stand now, she'll be a wealthy girl when I die because she's the only family I have. But I don't need you to baby sit or make sure a shotgun wedding takes place."

"You don't need this bastard at all, Joseph," the third man in the room broke in. "Damn it, man, for all we know he's already working for Luciano, and we've got Kincaid here."

I turned my head to look at him and shivered like a slimy worm was crawling up my back. Nick Pappas affected people like that. To me, he looked like a cross between the squat form of an Asian Buddha and a toad—a toad that had been locked up in a dark place for a long time. He'd been sitting in a chair at the window on my right, silent as a snake while he fingered my .38. He wasn't particularly tall, maybe five nine, but he was big, with a thick neck and a heavy jowled face. His hair had thinned out to greasy black strings which didn't cover the shiny dome anymore. His eyes peered at you from the back of tunnels of fat. He looked as though wherever he'd spent his life sunshine had been in short ration and the transparent pink of his skin would never tan. It gave him a dead, unhealthy look.

He wasn't the born rich type of tough. He was to Cardinalli what Goering was to Hitler. A crude slob who'd started at the bottom and worked his way up to Cardinalli's side, buying men happily along the way with a few well placed whispers. There was an ugly-looking scar on his forehead, red on the pale skin, and his ears looked like well hammered pieces of beef. They looked better than his lips though, which reminded me of two raw oysters. His looks and his methods of doing business made him one cat that few men wanted to cross. For all I knew, Cardinalli might keep him around just to scare hell out of wayward thugs. He was Cardinalli's chief little helper.

I took it all in and managed to grin tightly. "Hi, slob," I said. "Who turned over your rock?"

He pointed my .38 at my stomach. "Him we don't need, Joseph," he said again. "There's a thousand punks like him on the street."

Cardinalli slammed his hand down on the desk. "Shut up!" he barked. "I'll decide what we need! You already brought Kincaid in before telling me. Now let me decide what in hell we need."

He glared around the room in the silence which lasted several minutes. "All right," he said finally. "I've got a job for you, Judas. That's why you're here. I wanted you off the streets before one of Luciano's men saw you."

"If they didn't plant him on us," Kincaid said helpfully.

Cardinalli waved him off and asked me, "What do you know about Luciano and his bunch?"

I settled back in the chair, feeling the effects of the drug wearing off. "Not a hell of a lot," I admitted. "He's big in a small way because he has managed to worm his way into the rackets in a lot of cities. I'd say he's a careful bastard to play like that. He grabs just enough of the action so that not any single syndicate family considers him a real threat. They may not like his parasitic type of nibbling at the action, but individually the capos don't see him as a threat that's worth all the heat which pushing him out or killing him would bring." I paused and let that part soak in for a moment. "But you take all of Luciano's little pieces of action and add them together, and you realize that he's grabbed himself a big piece of action over the years. That's what you're fighting now, Cardinalli—all those little pieces combined, and they're likely in places where he can hurt you. I think Luciano has decided that he's strong enough for a big grab, and you're about the biggest he can go for. I don't think he likes you either, for that matter. So you're the target, Cardinalli, the boss capo."

Cardinalli stared at me for a long moment before he said, "You're almost right, Judas, almost. I wish to hell that his target had been me. I wish it had. . . ."

He let the sentence trail off, and I could feel the silence creep into the room. I was beginning to pick up the drift of Cardinalli's problem then. I wasn't making any guesses, but most of the big racket heads around could be put into a two-way bind that was really a beauty when you looked at it. If you understood the protocol involved in being a Mafia capo, you had a lever to put the squeeze on good. If was also enough to make you puke when you knew that putting the squeeze on always hurt someone outside the rackets, like killing a man's dog just to watch him squirm. It didn't take any great brain to figure out that Cardinalli was getting the squeeze put on him, but it was likely his daughter who was feeling the hand behind that squeeze. It was a question of who came first, Mafia or his daughter. That sort of problem is also one that outside help should stay to hell away from—unless, of course, the price is right.

"I don't like the sound of that, Cardinalli," I told him. "You don't even need to tell me why you brought me here because I can guess. Luciano is likely using your daughter to get at you. Maybe he wants you to hold still while he takes another cut of the action. Whatever the hell he's doing, you can't hold still for it because you took the oath." I grinned at him. "The Mafia comes first, don't it?"

"Keep talking," he grunted. "Let's see how goddamn smart you really are."

"I'm smart enough so that I never went through the bullshit of saying that I'd hold the rackets above everything; including my family, if I had a family. What the hell is the oath? 'We represent La Cosa Nostra, this family is our thing', isn't it? Well your thing has gotten you an ass full of trouble that I can't help you with. I'm not here to play bodyguard for any seventeen year old twitch. It's not my bag."

"A bodyguard I don't need," he said. "That isn't the job. I could use Kincaid for it if it was."

"You can suit yourself. I wouldn't use Kincaid to guard a whorehouse. But whatever stinking job you have in mind, I don't want any part of it. I take contracts, Cardinalli, not jobs that can tie me up for months."

"Suppose I say that Luciano's the contract?"

"Then we'll talk," I said. "Is he the job?"

"Not exactly, but he's part of it. We'll talk anyway, Judas," he said flatly and pulled another cigar from the box on his desk. "You're going to do this little job for me because you already know too much for me to let you go running around the streets where Luciano might hire you." He paused to light the cigar. "Either you work for me or you don't work, period."

I stared at the .38 in Pappas' hand and knew what he meant.

"Do we understand each other?"

"Yeah," I said. "You come through clear enough. What's the job?"

He settled back in the chair and looked thoughtful. "I've already told you that I don't need a bodyguard for Sandy," he said. "And you've guessed right that Luciano is using her to get at me."

I shook my head, thinking maybe Kincaid had slipped me another micky. "Then what?"

I watched him for a moment and finished my drink. It was going to be a long night. For some reason, kidnapping in Sicily is damn near a national sport. It appeared that Luciano had brought the time honored profession into practice in the good old U. S. Evidently he wasn't bothered about bending American laws for a snatch job. But then, you couldn't find fault with his views, since Cardinalli obviously wasn't going to call in the FBI's finest to get his daughter back. And it figured also that he wasn't going to shed one drop of Luciano's blood while there was a chance of getting his daughter back alive. That's where I came in.

Kidnappers, even those of the Mafia, work in a sort of set pattern. They could actually have killed the girl within hours after the snatch, knowing all along that Cardinalli would have to take their word for her being alive or dead. And too, after seeing a picture of Sandy in her bathing suit and knowing Luciano by reputation, they just might keep her around for entertainment. And last, it was even remotely possible that they would let the girl go if they got what they wanted. Unfortunately for Sandy, her capo father had no intention of meeting the demands of ransom.

"He wants control of the gambling rackets," Cardinalli was telling me. "I move my boys out, and he takes over, game rooms, number rackets, the bookies, the whole works. He'll release Sandy then."

I took my time lighting a cigarette and let my still misty mind work on that some. If he believed Luciano would release her, I wouldn't be here.

"All right," I said, ignoring Kincaid and Pappas. "So you give up a little piece of the gambling action in each city. He can't handle it all. What the hell, Cardinalli, what that will cost you won't hurt so much you'll bleed to death."

Pappas grunted like a hog in his chair and said, "A million a year we'd be handing him, a cool million. And what chance do you think there is of his turning her loose?"

"Why not?" I wanted to know. "What's his motive for killing the kid? He's already told you that he has her so he wouldn't kill her to shut her up. And he damn sure must know you'll put a contract on him, no matter if she turns up dead or alive. So what does he gain by killing her?"

Cardinalli took a long pull of his drink and fired up his cigar again. I could see him picking his brains for some reason to give me that I'd understand.

He waved his hand and shook his head. "Lucianos and Cardinallis," he said softly. "Since the old country, thert's been killing between the families. An old vendetta that ends with me because I don't have a son. With me the Cardinalli name stops. But that's not enough for Luciano, I don't think. With Sandy, the blood line would stop too, and he would have a complete revenge. That would be Luciano's way."

I shrugged. "I'm not up on your phony credos or the vendetta bit. Your best chance of keeping her alive is to give the bastard what he wants."

"I can't do that," Cardinalli said. "I alone don't make decisions that affect the syndicate. All the capos decide together."

"And they decided no deal, huh?"

Cardinalli spread his hands. "They decided what was best for the family," he paused, watching me. "No deal."

"Nice friends you've got," I told him and glanced at Pappas, who was smiling slightly. "It must be nice to know that the rackets are more important than your kid. You've got a stinking code to live by, Cardinalli."

Pappas' face twisted into a tight mask. "That code, as you call it, has held the family together. There are no exceptions to it, and the family comes first for all of us."

"Goody for you," I said. "I still think it stinks. But if it's all decided, what am I here for?"

Cardinalli wiped his face. "Nothing says that I can't try to get Sandy back before I tell Luciano no. For that I need someone Luciano doesn't know. You have a better chance of finding her than any of my own men."

Pappas was watching me critically, running his eyes

over me like I was a prime steak, while his head wagged in disagreement. "I don't think we should trust him, Joseph."

Cardinalli shrugged it off. "You want the contract, Judas?"

"Have I got a choice?"

"No."

I nodded. "I'll give it a try for ten thousand, Cardinalli. Half when I start, the rest when I finish. And I do it my way." Pappas' mouth went tight when I grinned at him. "Any of your boys show up while I'm looking, and I'll bury them."

Cardinalli's eyes went half closed as he studied me. After a moment he said, "That's the way you'd have to do it, Judas, because I don't know who's siding with Luciano in this. But I don't trust you that much either, so Kincaid here goes along to make sure you don't find a higher bidder. Neither of you are syndicate, so it shouldn't tip them off."

I stared at Kincaid across the room, not liking it a bit. "Okay," I shrugged. "Just make sure he stays out of my hair. Clue me in on how they made the snatch. Where do I start?"

CHAPTER TWO

I started with a name, five thousand dollars in my pocket and the prospect of Kincaid tagging my heels like a loving brother. The name that Cardinalli had given me was Nino. That's all, just Nino, and the address of the bar where I would find him. It was a good place to start earning my ten grand, since Nino was a fringe member of Luciano's little gathering of followers who'd decided that the feel of some long green was worth passing on a bit of information, or so Cardinalli said. But at the moment, I wasn't putting any heavy money on anything that Cardinalli said.

That's the beauty of a syndicate contract. When you take one, they figure they've bought you, and you couldn't be sure what extra plans a man like Cardinalli could have for you. There was no getting around the fact that with Pappas and Kincaid around, a job could get hairy. I knew I was figured to be a piece of something more than just finding the girl. The trick would be to find out what part I was slated to play. It all seemed very simple: just find out where they were keeping the girl and get her back if I could. But the contract stank, because I knew things weren't likely to work out that way. Everything was out of focus, starting with the damned sketchy information I'd been given to start with. And those reasons I *had* been given were doubtful when you looked at them. There should be a good reason behind Luciano's play, and money wasn't quite good enough. Hell, a man doesn't risk a sure slug in the head and a shallow grave for something he wouldn't live to enjoy. At least he didn't do that unless he had some cards to play that Cardinalli didn't know about—or at least wasn't telling me about. I felt the skin on my back crawl as I headed for the cab stand down the street.

Something had happened to the city while I chatted with Cardinalli. There wasn't any glow left in the neon for me, and the shadows between the buildings pulled my eyes to probe for shapes among them. I was hunting again. Grinning to myself, I flagged a cab down, gave the driver a Maxwell Street address and settled back in the seat to think about Nino.

A Maxwell Street address wasn't expected to be a place where you go for the charm and atmosphere. I wasn't disappointed in that expectation when I paid off the cab a half block away from the address I wanted and picked my way up a sidewalk where garbage had been tossed from the crumbling tenements. I couldn't really decide whether the area was Chicago's garbage dump or a sort of standing museum dedicated to the good old days. It sure as hell wasn't Madison Avenue. I walked around a happy alcoholic who hadn't quite made it to the gutter before he'd passed out. The .38 felt good under my arm because I felt like a new bug crawling into the city's open sore.

Like Maxwell Street wasn't Madison Avenue, Max's Bar wasn't any Playboy Club either. The place was crowded between a drugstore and an all-night diner, both of which sported a small gathering of punks who looked like SS troops taking a break from a blitzkrieg of the city. The entrance to Max's sported its own drunk sleeping in front of the door. By the smell of him, he'd missed the can somewhere during the evening. I pushed open the painted green door and stopped a few steps inside to let my eyes adjust to the bar lights.

The place would have gotten a three D rating in anyone's book. It was damp, dark and dirty, and it smelled like a pot party in a sewer. In the dim light I checked out the weed-heads blowing grass in the booths and the boozers holding up the bar. I wondered which group Nino would be doing his thing with.

The bartender was fat and sloppy. He grunted his way down to me to splash vodka and water into a glass when I ordered. Then he slid the glass over to me and waited for his money.

I dropped a five on the bar, kept my hand on it and asked, "Is Nino around?"

He deadpanned me and fingered the edge of the bill.

"Who wants to know?" he asked.

"I do, friend," I told him and showed him a lot of teeth in a smile. "Either he's here or he isn't. That shouldn't be hard even for you to figure out."

He tried to stare me to death and gave it up, saying, "We don't want any trouble here, pal. What's Nino to you?"

"A talk," I said and took my hand away from the five.

"Sure, Nino's around," he said casually. "He haunts this place, and I never saw anything but trouble from him."

"Do I look like trouble?"

He grunted and pocketed the five. "Yeah. You sure as hell do," he said. "So if you give this dump trouble, I'm calling the law."

"You do that, friend. Where's Nino?"

The bartender shrugged and waved a hand toward the rear of the place. That's him in the last booth."

Nino was sitting still as a stone, hunched over his drink like he was worried someone might take it. I nodded to the bartender and crossed the no man's land between the bar and the booths and slid in across the table from Nino.

Nino was one of those guys you see standing in the shadows near the action, like a hyena showing up after the kill. Guys like Nino are what cops use to beef up their statistics when they pull in a dragnet. One look and I knew there was enough pressure on to make him scared. I also knew there was more than me around for him to be scared of. He took a quick look at my face and glanced furtively around the bar.

"All right, Nino. Cardinalli says he's buying. So what have you got to sell?"

He grabbed a nervous cigarette from the pack next to his glass and lit it with a hand that shook. "Jesus Christ," he said, "I can't talk here like I'm a Cardinalli man."

"I like it here, Nino," I told him, "so talk."

His mouth got tight. He tried to watch everyone in the place at once. "Why borrow trouble? Let's go to my pad."

"I'm a new face, Nino." I smiled and watched him squirm. "You can always say I'm an old pal from reform school or something."

"Man," he hissed, "that won't wash at all. They had you pegged the Judas and Cardinalli's man two hours ago. The description fits, too."

"Who's got me pegged?"

His face sagged as he looked around some more. "Everyone. You ain't good company to be seen with, that's all."

I studied him for a few moments while I worked on my drink. He had scare pasted all over his face. You could smell the fear leaking out of him as he sat there.

I leaned forward and tapped him on the hand. "Then spill it and run, creep," I said. "What do you have about Cardinalli's kid?"

He cringed slightly and looked ready to bolt until he remembered money and said, "She's alive, man. They got her tucked away because Luciano wants her old man to hear her talk if he gives them trouble."

"Where's she at?"

"How much is Cardinalli paying for this?"

"Enough," I said and handed over the envelope I'd brought with me. "Now where's she at?"

He clutched the envelope and slid to the end of the booth, glancing around the room again. Then he leaned across and whispered to me like a James Bond spy.

"I ain't got that, man. Those bastards aren't telling no one that, but Billy Swan was one of them in on the snatch; he'd know. He's got a shack-up over at 1500 Jackson, her name's Lynch. Maybe he's laying up there too." He glanced around the room once more, then said, "You're hot, man. Real hot." With that, my gutless friend left the place like he knew it was going to be raided.

I rubbed my forehead and toyed with my drink, thinking I'd just spent five hundred of Cardinalli's money to get myself right back where I'd been when I came into the dive. I had a name to look for and a big city to do it in. Knowing Cardinalli's daughter was alive didn't help one hell of a lot because I had the feeling that the word had gotten out too fast for the job to be what you could call an easy contract. I had to think so when a guy like Nino already had the word on me and could name the side I was working for. True, someone might have seen me taken out of the bar by Cardinalli's men and done a little guessing from that. There was also the cheerful prospect of a double-cross in the works. I wondered where Kincaid was and just who was doing the hunting on this contract.

I ordered another drink, watched the weed-heads

tripping out in the other booths and listened to the growl of the city. There were a few million people packed together with their troubles outside. I was supposed to be interested in just one—just one caught in the middle of a thing called Mafia, where she was a pawn for Luciano. That's how the game was played, feeding off anything it touched. It was a game that caused fear and made widows, but it ran continuously because it had too much money behind it.

Put a seventeen year old twitch into that, and you couldn't laugh it off. Not when you knew how quick a pawn was dead when it wasn't useful any longer. That was another code Luciano and Cardinalli lived by: once the Mafia fingered you, it only turned you loose one way—dead. Sandy wasn't worth ten grand to me dead.

I waited until a name came to mind. Then I traded the smell of marijuana and booze for the stink of the city outside. I stood under the bar light in front of the building and took my time lighting a cigarette while I checked the area for Kincaid, who didn't seem to be doing his bird-dogging very well. I didn't have time to feel lonesome because the guy in front of the greasy spoon next door seemed ready to take a walk without knowing which way he wanted to go. I went west up Maxwell and helped him make up his mind. He was a half block behind me at the first street light.

I picked the dark side of the street from there on to make it easier for him because someone wasn't listening right. I'd agreed to Kincaid's tagging me, but that was all. Who needed an idiot Mafia disciple around to advertise my affiliation? I picked up the pace in the dark and walked past a few alleys like I was moving scared and I had him practically breathing on my neck in three blocks. Then I cut one more alley and waited for him.

He was young and eager, with an executive look

which made him a well dressed punk with a thin wallet and an urge to earn himself a name. He was already in the alley before he sorted me out from the dark and the garbage cans and began digging in his coat for something to point at me. I kicked him in the crotch before he could get the gun out. Then he was gagging among the garbage cans.

I took the flat automatic out of his pocket and tossed its clip down the alley before I dropped the gun down into the mess he'd made. Then I gave him a look at the barrel of my .38 pointed about two inches from his eye. I told him, "You better get yourself a new job, baby. And tell Cardinalli not to send any more of you to watch me. One is enough."

He looked at me with watery eyes and kept holding his crotch while he tried to come up with a punch line. He settled for, "Screw Cardinalli."

I thumped him in the head and walked off with a dry sour taste in my mouth. There was more than vagueness to the job now. There were some unexplained facts—like Luciano knowing I was working already. Nino had known it, college boy back there in the alley had been sent to do something about it, both knowing more than they should on a job that wasn't four hours old. Also, I wasn't at all happy about the closed mouthed characteristics of Cardinalli and his helpers. Someone was running his mouth like a stoolie trying to build his retirement fund.

I found a cab two blocks away and then changed cabs twice more on my way across town. I didn't want a tail on this visit. Like Cardinalli said, it was going to take someone the rackets didn't know to get any lead on the girl, and it was going to take someone who had the connections to put an ear on the grapevine too. I only knew one man who could fit into that. True, the local talent had once known him well enough to look over their shoulder when he was operating, but that was a long time ago, and hopefully even the Mafia forgets. I hoped that they had forgotten about Red Butcher because I knew that he would remember them real good. Pure cold hate can sometimes get you more cooperation than money.

There are all kinds of cops in Chicago. Red Butcher used to be one of the good ones. He used to be a lot of things before he had a run in with the Mafia on a case and got a dose of crooked politics to top it off.

He met me at the door to his apartment with a newspaper in his hand. He stared at my face for a long while before recognition came into his eyes and he said, "A long time, Judas."

We shook hands, not quite friends, both of us knowing that the other brought trouble when he came around. He waved me into the one chair in the room and sat down on the bed.

"What brings you to Chicago?" he asked.

"I like the climate."

"Bullshit. You never went any place in your life if it didn't have money and Mafia involved. And right now you're on top of the shit heap."

"Word gets around fast."

"You don't know how fast. Even at the dump where I tend bar, I heard about your being chosen for Cardinalli. I was worried."

"That helps," I told him.

"Now I wish someone had given you a train ticket and pointed you south while they had you."

He fished around on the night stand by the bed and came up with a cigarette while he studied me. "You're here and you're working. Poison."

"For you too, Red?"

He tried to grin, but the twisted scar tissue that covered most of his face pulled his mouth into a sneer. "There's no cop left in me, Judas," he said. "What you do with your gun doesn't bother me."

"It shouldn't. You pulled the trigger a few times yourself, didn't you? From behind a badge, wasn't it?" I asked. "Only it got you busted off the force as a thank you from the city. That was Mafia too, buddy, the boys who have this city right by the nuts."

Nothing changed in his face. "That was a long time ago, Judas. Just like my face was a long time ago."

I could see him remembering while I rubbed his raw spot. "They shot a friend of yours to get you off their back. And then they gave you a face lifting with acid, wasn't that it, Lieutenant? So you strapped on your .38 and pushed two of them when the law said you didn't get to be judge, jury and executioner behind that badge."

"Shut up, Judas."

His mouth was tight. I had a funny feeling that I could only push him so far before his hate started to include me.

"You did your shooting for a friend," I said. "I do mine for money. Nobody can fire me, Butcher."

"Okay, I'm impressed."

"I'm not trying to impress you. I'm trying to find out if you want to help me screw up some more of our friends."

"Like who?"

"How about Luciano to start with?"

He worked at another distorted grin. "Go ahead," he said. "It could be interesting. But if you're looking for help, take a good look. Tough guys can be found all over the docks. An old tough one you don't need."

I took my time and looked at him then. He was still a big man, getting a bit soft in the stomach and gray in the hair, but still big, and his pale skin and soft hands from years behind a bar couldn't take that away. He could have been four feet tall, and he would have still been big when you looked in his eyes. If you'd known him before, it was like seeing a played out shell of what they once called a real hard one. His eyes, however, said there was one part of him which wasn't dead. The flat, cold hate was still there in Butcher.

That was all he needed to make him dangerous. People sometimes get the idea that a dangerous man can only be a big one who's got a hardcase style to everything he does. A few times they can be right, but most of the deadly ones don't look at all deadly. They are the ones who know how to kill you and will do it while they look like they're on their way to a PTA meeting. So Butcher could look like anything, as long as he carried that hate in his eyes and the scar on his face.

"Okay," I said. "I'm looking. Now, do you want to play with some dirty marbles or not?"

He thought for a moment, then nodded. "You wouldn't come to me if you needed an extra gun. That's for sure. So how much leg work and what kind of questions do I ask?"

"You catch the drift real quick, Red."

He worked at a smile again. "I used to be a cop, didn't I? You got a bad one on your mind, and I'm a special source of information. Let's hear what you want."

I shrugged. "I'm not too damn sure. Cardinalli and Luciano are the ones I need information on."

"Who is paying you?"

"Cardinalli," I said. "A snatch job, and Luciano is using his daughter to put the squeeze on. This contract stinks, but I can't see where the smell is coming from."

He whistled silently. "A nice dirty one you got," he agreed. "Tell me the rest."

It took me fifteen minutes to run it down. Meanwhile, he picked the events apart like a cop at a grilling session and then said, "You need a leg man all right. With Luciano wise and Kincaid as your helper, you're not going to be able to fart without someone calling his boss about it." He found himself a cigarette and lit it.

"You're going to be the target while I dig, you know. Luciano will work at keeping you away—or dead."

"That's the idea," I said. "It will keep him busy. How about Billy Swan? Know anything about him?"

"Some," he said casually. "He's a Luciano man, all right. The usual local hood. Chicago boy, not much over twenty right now. He's had a police record since he was twelve."

"He still living with the Lynch girl over on Jackson?"

"Maybe. It's worth checking, but his being in on that snatch doesn't sound right."

"How do you figure?"

"Look at it like this. Sure, he gets paid by Luciano now, but before this trouble started he ran with the same bunch as the Cardinalli kid did." He paused. "So he likely knew the girl. Hell, he wasn't a part of either family, so a problem between Luciano and Cardinalli wouldn't stop him there—no phony vendetta code to bind him."

"Until Luciano put him on the payroll and really started to push Cardinalli, you mean."

"Yeah. Then they drew the lines and Luciano's men had to stay out of Cardinalli territory. I'd still say that he knew the girl."

I grunted and pulled my tie loose. "That's likely the reason he was used on the snatch."

"I'll check it," Butcher said. "He's young, and he could be a weak link to this." He watched me, then made a decisive shrug with his shoulders. "I'll check it, and you can lean on him. Let's give that angle a spin and see what happens."

"You still have an ear in down at the station?" I asked.

"I've still got friends on the force, if that's what you're asking. They don't like Mafia any more than I do. What's in that for you?"

"Information. Like I said, there's a smell about this one I don't like. Some of the blue coated wonders' theories on the current racket trend might turn up what it is before I do, because they're seeing it from a different angle. I don't care where I get it, just so the information covers these two and Pappas."

"What's with Pappas? A personal grudge?"

"Let's say he wasn't eager to have me take the contract."

Butcher nodded. "He wouldn't be if he had Kincaid lined up for that—his pet killer from what I hear." He paused and nodded again. "We still come up with one important question first. Where are they keeping the girl? That's going to be a touchy subject for anyone to dig up."

I grinned at him. "There's one more important question," I told him. "I'd like to know what Luciano's going to do to keep me from finding her."

"You won't have any problem in getting an answer for that," he said. "All you need is go out and look. Are you going to start with Billy Swan?"

I pushed myself out of my chair and stretched. "First Swan's girl. If he happens to be shacked up when I get there, it'll be even better."

Butcher picked up his shirt from the bed and started pulling it on. "There's not much to start on," he said, "but I think I'll do a little visiting myself tonight. I don't like the idea of Luciano having the girl, even if she is Cardinalli's kid."

"I'll be around," I told him.

"And Judas?"

I stopped at the door. "Yeah?"

"I want in on the finish, okay?"

I watched his eyes a moment and nodded.

That's how information for a contract can be dug out of the city. You ask, and you pay, and sometimes you break an arm or such. But always, you use people like Butcher with his hate, and eventually there will be a fact or event that puts you closer to the payoff. You try not to think about the people you're using, but you always wonder who'll play the final card.

I thought about Billy Swan's girl as I found a cab.

CHAPTER THREE

The city was abloom with neon as the cab took me back to the hotel on Chicago Avenue. Something happens to a city at night when the dark hides its plain-faced grime. It puts on an evening dress of light and throbs out the come-on to the suckers with a voice that's never still, and it's a round heel that will take you every time.

I left the cab a block from my hotel and walked amid the night sounds, looking for Kincaid. Two hours had passed. He should be getting nervous about losing me. It figured that he would wait, watching the hotel until he could pick me up again.

I found him sitting behind a newspaper in the lobby when I stopped at the desk for my key. He didn't look much like a killer then; he looked more like he was gay and geared for a date with a truck driver. His eyes narrowed to thin slits which matched his mouth when he got up to follow me upstairs.

He switched to a meaningless smile when he found a

chair by the bed. He made a production of lighting a cigarette like he had all the time in the world, but there wasn't any patience showing in his eyes. They seemed to be all you noticed in his thin face. Like two bugs on a blank sheet of paper.

The patient act went on until I said, "Nino gave me five hundred bucks worth of nothing."

His smile got real then. "Not quite," he said. "He sold you enough to get himself put face down in the gutter. He was dead as a stone when I saw him last." He licked his lips like he had enjoyed the sight.

"You do it?" I asked.

He shook his head. "They were waiting for him when he came out. I tagged along behind to see it happen. He must have slipped somewhere and tipped Luciano."

"He leaked more than that," I said. "Someone was waiting for me too."

Kincaid didn't look worried. "So we got to sweat a bit now. Not a chance of playing it quiet."

I studied his smile from across the room. "*I've* got Luciano to sweat, friend. You're just along for the ride, remember?"

He shrugged it off. His smile faded like it was too much work holding it. "I don't suppose you'll tell me what Nino did have to say?"

"A name. Billy Swan. What do you know about him?"

"I'm new here myself, remember?" The smirk came back. "Besides, you don't want me to do your work, do you?"

"Knock it off, punk, before I remember I don't like you. Want to see Cardinalli's kid back? I want the same thing, and if we start getting in each other's way, nobody gets anything." I grinned back at him then. "Except maybe you could get dead."

His fingers broke the cigarette in half as his hands

clenched. It took him a full minute before he trusted himself to talk again.

"All right," he said. "I just don't know anything about Swan, except that he's with Luciano."

I kept watching him, waiting for his expression to change. "Sure," I said softly. "I wonder how many others around here are with Luciano. Somebody tipped them that I was in this, friend."

His eyes kept a bland expression. I hated his guts, and he knew it, yet his years as a pro made him nearly expressionless. "That could be," he said easily. "What do you do now?"

"I keep digging like Luciano didn't know. The contract doesn't let me out if the cards aren't stacked right."

"It could take a lot of time."

"I've got a lot of time."

His eyes were satisfied and deadly. "Maybe you've got a week," he said. "No more. After that, Cardinalli tells Luciano to go to hell and puts his own guns on him. If you screw up the contract, he might send one after you, too."

"It's not enough time."

"Make it enough," Kincaid said. "You're only useful until Luciano knows there's no deal. Then Cardinalli might stop worrying about your health."

"But you won't, huh?"

"That's right," he said and stood up. "I don't happen to like you either, Judas. You screwed me out of a contract."

"I'll watch my back," I told him as he went to the door.

"Do that." He tapped his hat and gave me a killing look. "I'll be around."

I stared at the door after he had left and knew that he damn sure would be around. The thought made my back itch.

Outside, the city was drawing into itself with the late

hour. Some of the neon was out and the doorways chained. It was too late to start any social calls or night life. For me, the time could be just right.

If Swan was spending any time with his shack-up, he should be there now. With a late cab, I found the address. I got inside the entranceway of the building and started looking for the name Frances Lynch over the mailboxes. After my fifth match, I dug the address out of my pocket and checked it again. Then I started swearing when another match showed me an empty slot over one box. I pushed the buzzer for that one for five minutes and gave it up. It wasn't turning out to be my day at all. I stood in the dark and thought about Nino selling the address like it was worth something and then pushed the button labeled "CARETAKER." The door clicked, and I went in.

The building was the usual firetrap, a hangover from the good old days. Even its money grubbing owner seemed to realize that no amount of paint and patching would keep it standing. There hadn't been any visible repairs on the place in years. The musty dampness of the rotting building stuck in my throat.

I found the caretaker's room at the end of the hall and pounded on his door until someone eased it open a night chain's three inches, and a bloodshot eyeball glared out at me. From what I could see, the caretaker was a thin whisper of a man who wore a dirty shirt and grimy trousers. I nodded at the eye peering at me and said, "Where's Frances Lynch? She had 14B, front."

"I know what she had," he snapped. "I collect the rent here, don't I?" He glared at me like I was a building inspector and added, "What the hell do you want, coming around this time of night?"

"I'm looking for the Lynch girl."

"All right, go and look then. Don't be beating on my door."

"Her name's not over the mailbox any more."

He was silent for a moment while he slid the night

chain off and opened the door. "I don't know nothing about that," he said. "Maybe she took off." He waved a hand. "I just collect the rent, see? What people do around here is their own business. All I know is that her rent's paid until the end of the month."

I dug my wallet out and let my fingers do the talking with the bills. "Let's go check her room, huh?"

He hesitated, eying the wallet. "You a friend of hers?"

"Yeah," I lied. "I want to know why her name's not on the mailbox." I fingered a twenty half way out of my wallet and waited.

He hesitated a little more, then picked a ring of keys off a nail beside the door. "Wouldn't hurt to check, I guess. Your being a friend and all."

He had the twenty in his pocket when we went up the two flights. He keyed open the door, felt around for the light switch and turned the lights on before stepping aside.

I had no idea at all what I expected to find. There were just too many coincidences happening for me to like it. Nino was dead from giving me Swan's name, and now Swan's girl was gone. By the looks of the apartment, she had left in one hell of a hurry, too.

The place was a typical thread-bare apartment without trimmings. It had a kitchen and living room combined with bedroom next to the bath. The furniture was worn and stained but not with any of the stains I was half expecting. After Nino, I knew that murder would be catching. It just naturally leads to more murder.

I glanced at the odds and ends of clothing scattered around the rooms and walked into the bedroom. The closet was open and empty. The dresser top was bare.

"Looks like you lost a roomer, pal."

He didn't look very surprised about it and stood there watching me go through the dresser drawers. There was nothing there at all. I pushed a cigarette between my lips and lit it before I asked, "All right, pal, when did she leave?"

"I told you, her rent's paid."

"I know damn well what you told me," I said. "But no twitch is going to pack up and leave right under your nose without you knowing about it."

Jerking his eyes away from mine, he began to fumble with the keys. "Mister," he said, "I can't keep track of who comes and goes in this dump. Her rent was paid. That's all I worry about. If you're a friend of hers, you should know where she went."

I leaned against the door and grinned. "I will as soon as you tell me."

There was a worried look on his face, like he didn't care for the idea of being in a room with me. He jerked his eyes around some more and ran his tongue over his lips. "Aw, come off it, Mister. If she's got herself another boyfriend, leave her be. There's plenty of dames around."

"Is that what she told you? She moved because her boyfriend was bothering her?"

"I guess so," he said. "She just packed up and went."

"How about her address? She left that, didn't she?"

He sucked in a deep breath and eyed the door as he let it out in a sigh. "Goddamn dames," he said. "She probably wanted you to find her anyway. They like to be chased."

"I'm not chasing, friend," I said, handing him a pen and paper. "Just write it down."

He eyed me for a moment, considered what he owed ex-roomers and started writing. Then he handed over the address. "That's where she said to send her mail. Her problems ain't any concern of mine. She didn't want anyone getting that though."

I pocketed the address. "She'll want me to know it," I said and grinned at him. "What does she look like?"

"You said you knew her!"

I stared at him and kept grinning.

"All right! All right! She's a stacked blonde, about five foot four. Green eyes, I think. Now get the hell out of here."

I nodded. "I'll find her. But don't make the same mistake twice and give out that address to anyone else. You know what I mean?"

He looked away and swallowed a couple of times. He knew what I meant all right. He couldn't miss the dull gleam of my .38 which had been showing since I unbuttoned my jacket to get the cigarette. Sometimes it's best to just let them decide for themselves what the gun is there for.

The new address he'd given me was over on Division Avenue. If anything, the girl had gone from bad to worse when she changed pads. This one was on the second floor over a bar that provided background music. The only window in the room was directly above the blinking beer sign. With those advantages, it wasn't exactly a restful room. All the mailboxes in the entranceway had yellowed name tags except the F. Lynch one. I knew this was my traveling twitch.

Pushing the room buzzer a few times, I enjoyed the dark and the stink of the bar next door. Then I sighed, punched the whole row and slid into the shadows of the stairway at the first buzz. It was even darker inside. I waited with the garbage cans and the smell of urine until my eyes adjusted to the light.

It wasn't any lighter in the hallway upstairs, but the bar light outside kept giving me brief red flashes to find the room. I listened a moment before I rapped on the door and caught the creak of bed springs as someone moved inside.

All I got for my knocking was silence. I knocked again, then rattled the knob. Finally, I poked my own room key into the lock and toyed with that before moving back down the hall.

There wasn't any doubt in my mind that the girl in

the room was good and scared then, and I was betting on that fear to make her move next. I checked my watch and decided that it would be at least a half an hour before anything happened, so I backed into the deeper shadows of the next doorway to wait.

It was twenty minutes before a light went on in the room and showed a thin edge under the door, and another seven minutes passed before the lady decided to come out. She was in a hurry. She jerked the door shut behind her, clutched her purse under her arm and took the few steps that put her in front of me. I heard her rapid breathing and let her go past before I stepped out and got a head hold with my left arm, covering her mouth at the same time. I let her writhe as I locked my hands together to pull her against me. I used the leverage of both my wrists and put pressure on her neck. It takes about half a minute if you do it right. If you do it wrong, you wind up with a corpse.

I held her a moment after her body went slack and then carried her back to her room. She was, as the caretaker had said, a nicely stacked little bundle. I dumped her onto the bed, wondered where her boyfriend was and sat down to wait.

Her eyes were green all right, but they were glazed with fear when she came to. She let her gaze crawl over me slowly, but she didn't scream. Maybe she knew that it wouldn't have done her any good. I shook out a smoke and offered her one, saying, "You should answer your doorbell when you have visitors."

"That was you before? At the door?"

"Yeah. Were you expecting someone else?"

She stayed quiet, and her hand shook as she took the cigarette.

"Whoever you were expecting doesn't matter. If I'd wanted you hurt, you wouldn't be here now, right?"

She didn't move. "What do you want?"

"A talk," I said. "I'm looking for Billy Swan because I want a talk with him, too."

She blinked at me. "More."

"No more to it. The name is Jones. I picked up your name and Swan's and followed you over here from your old pad. If anyone else is looking for you, they can come the same way."

"That goddamn super," she said. "I've got to move again now."

"Why?" I wanted to know.

"Because I'm not that creep's girl any more. I told him that when he told me about . . ." She bit it off.

I grinned at her. "About his being in on grabbing the Cardinalli kid, huh?"

Her eyes widened, then grew blank with fear again. "Who are you?"

"Kid," I sighed, "it's been a long night for me, and I'm a little bewildered about what's going on just now. I'm also goddamn tired of running around this city without learning anything I need. But whoever I am, I'm not anyone you're scared of. So we can do this any way you like. I'm going to ask some questions, and I'm going to beat hell out of you if I don't get some answers. Now, what'll it be?"

The fear and hardness stayed in her eyes as she sighed, "Ask away."

"Where's Billy Swan for a start?"

She paused a moment. "I'm not sure now. If he's still in town, he's either at Luciano's or out at his cottage on the lake. I left as soon as he told me about the Cardinalli girl."

"Why?"

"I didn't want any part of that. Cardinalli will find out Billy was involved, and if they can't find him they'll look for me. I just don't want any part of it." Her eyes fastened on mine. "I'm scared, okay? I'm just plain scared."

"What did Swan tell you?"

"Just that Luciano was going to use the girl to get at Cardinalli. That's all! I didn't ask any more."

"Did he say where they had her?"

She shook her head. "Nothing. She was with them and that was all. Billy said he couldn't risk staying at the other apartment now. He knew Cardinalli would find out that he was in on it too and start looking for him."

"True love, huh?" I said. "He just walked out on you then?"

"It was over anyway." She said it very easily, like it had been over between them for a long time. "I saw someone watching the apartment when he left. I knew they would ask me about the girl too."

"So you packed up after lover boy went where the protection was. Why do that if you don't know anything?"

Her fear was a live thing over her face, and her hands clenched into tight balls, the nails biting into her palms. She knew why she'd done the moving. She had lived with Mafia, knew how they worked. She knew that they would work some on her—just to find out that she knew nothing.

Her hand moved up to her mouth. "I don't know anything," she whispered, "but they won't believe me if they find me. They won't believe me until . . ." She let it hang there unfinished and asked, "Have you ever seen what they do to someone to make them talk?"

I'd seen it. Shaking out a cigarette, I lit it while I tried to forget about seeing it. I looked at the fear in her face and remembered how easy she'd been to find. The only trouble with her thinking was that she was right. Cardinalli wouldn't be sitting still because I was working. He'd look for Swan, and he'd look for her, and he'd have someone like Kincaid ask questions until they were sure that she knew nothing. By then it wouldn't matter one way or the other for her. I didn't blame her for running.

"They won't be wanting to ask you anything if I find

Swan first," I said. "What about his beach cottage? Any chance that they're keeping the girl there?"

She shrugged. "I can tell you where it's at."

I reached out and unclenched her hands. They felt cold and still in mine. "You can show me better."

"I can't."

"No?" I asked. "You can always wait here for someone to come around with a few questions like I did. Only they'll ask them different." I shook my head. "Did you unpack yet?"

"Just a few things."

"Pack them back up."

She touched her lips with her tongue. "Where are we going?"

"My place," I said. "At least until they have a talk with Swan or I do. You'll be okay after that."

"Why?" she asked and watched my face.

"Maybe I don't like the son-of-a-bitch who's asking Cardinalli's questions for him. Maybe I'm just stupid. What difference does it make?" I waited. "Are you coming or not?"

She took all of a half minute to make up her mind. "I'm coming," she said and started packing.

The city had crawled back into itself in preparation for the morning by the time we reached the hotel. I checked the lobby for Kincaid and found only the night clerk sleeping behind the desk. He was still dozing peacefully as we went up the stairs.

It was all nice and easy. Upstairs I told her that she looked like hell and that she had better get some sleep. She smiled and stood close with her hands touching my face. "Sleep wasn't what I thought you had in mind," she said.

I let my hands rest on her hips and grinned. "I like the merchandise, but I'm too tired to get laid and enjoy it."

I sat in the chair by the window and watched the city come awake outside. One way or the other, I'd started the ball rolling. It would roll and bounce and pick up little bits of garbage out of people's lives until it finally stopped with me in the center of it.

Now they would hear about Swan's girl. They would wonder and worry some because they didn't know what she knew and because she was with me. They could tell themselves anything they wanted, but they couldn't ever be sure that she didn't know something that could hurt them.

I hoped it would make Luciano worry himself right into a mistake, because when he worried enough he might start thinking that Billy Swan was a mistake too, and he'd have to correct that. Like I said, murder is just naturally catching. This time I had some bait they would want.

Frances was sleeping soundly as the sun pushed its way up over the skyline, and I settled for a shower instead of some sleep to face the new day.

CHAPTER FOUR

It was a few minutes before ten that morning when I reached the neighborhood bar where Butcher put in his eight to four shift as a working square. I had spent the early hours finding a car rental and had picked out a blue Ford for transportation. I cruised the city some to check on a tail before finding my way to Butcher. I didn't like the idea that Kincaid again seemed to be off on some business of his own because whatever Kincaid did wouldn't help me any. I shrugged off the feeling and paid attention to what Butcher had collected from his night's work.

He set a cool beer in front of me and leaned on the bar. "Judas," he said, "you are one unpopular son-of-a-bitch."

"Tell me something new."

"They've spread it all over the street that you're out for Luciano," he went on. "Not a thing about the girl—just you, out on a kill contract for Cardinalli."

He paused. "I wonder who in hell has been doing your advertising."

"Bad?"

He nodded. "Let's put it like this. Wherever you go, you'll be poison. Someone already laid it on Luciano, and he's spending money on you already." He leaned against the back bar and laughed. "One guy and they're snaky out there. To make them worry like that, you got to be wading in a dirty puddle that's more than you've told me."

"Just the girl, Red," I told him. "That's all Cardinalli's paying for."

"I'll take a side bet right now that you're in more than you know then. What's making this much heat?"

I shrugged. "It could be that Luciano didn't expect someone like me. He was only worried about Cardinalli dealing and got me instead. Now he's in too deep to do much more than sweat out an answer. He'll have to walk easy and keep a lot of company around him. If he thinks this is only a kill contract, there's a chance for the girl yet." I grinned. "Let him worry about a contract; it's happened before."

"You've never had him trying to make you dead before."

"Who has he got on me?"

"Two local boys by the names of Bello and Potts. The best description I can hand you is off Thierney's files." He handed over a loosely scrawled rundown. I studied it for a moment and then asked, "New men at it?"

"They've buried a few, enough to be pros. A bad pair if they can set you up."

"So I'll let them set me up. Maybe I can pick the place. I can't dodge them on their own ground and look for the girl at the same time."

His grin grew a little wider as he slid another piece of paper onto the bar and waited while I read the address on it. "That's Swan's new apartment. He moved in there nice and quiet like a few days ago, likely when he came back from his little trip. He's been staying inside since then, so it's likely the hole he picked to crawl into."

I checked the address a second time and burned the paper in an ashtray. "How much did that cost you?"

"Just shoe leather," he said. "I know the beat cop in that neighborhood. He likes to keep track of the trouble that moves in on him. He made Swan while he was stocking up on smokes and was curious enough to check it."

He picked a cigar out of a box on the back bar and started to unwrap it. "Swan, finding a layup then, makes it sound like he was already walking scared before you got into this."

I read the question in the words and said, "Only of Cardinalli. Our friend Billy Swan was in on this snatch, Red."

"Where did you get that?"

"Swan's girl." I thought about that and added, "She was running too, before I came into it."

He put the cigar into his mouth and chewed at it without picking up a light. "It stinks," he said simply.

"Yeah, but tell me why though. Why me, if Cardinalli had already made up his mind?"

"You got dropped right in the middle of a rat race. Having Kincaid there makes it look like all they needed was someone to fill in a piece of a plan. Everything was already moving before you got there."

I waited.

"Cardinalli could need a fall man, you know. Only I can't see where yet. If he's just after Luciano, he's not needing anyone to hang a murder on. The bastard's got the money in the right places to cover a hit like that. I don't think he's dumb enough to believe you'd be an easy frame either. You've killed too many for that."

"They hire me to do it," I grinned. "No pay, no contract. It doesn't make me lose any sleep." I watched his eyes. "My so-called ghosts don't bother me like yours, Butcher."

He was good at covering it, but I caught the slight flicker his look held then, and I knew that I was rubbing his raw spot again. He was still a cop inside; he'd always be that.

I looked away, saying, "You could be right though. Cardinalli brought me in for more than his kid. If nothing else, he wants me to catch Luciano's heat while his own people look for the girl. That could explain why Luciano was told I was in this."

He waited, telling me with his eyes that he didn't buy that any more than I did, but he shrugged, "You know how many would like to collect a bonus on you?"

"One's too many," I told him. "But, I've got one thing their usual targets don't have. They know I'll play it as dirty as they can."

Butcher was letting his mind take him back to when he'd done his own shooting. It was all he had to remember. He shook it off with, "Better check on Swan. I'll see what I can dig up on Pappas."

"Dig up a burglar for me too," I said and put my hat on. "At least the tools. I might do a little house breaking tonight."

I could feel his eyes on my back as I left the bar.

The rock Billy Swan had picked to crawl under was in a row of flats on the North Side that was as desolate as an old whore. The building Swan was in had a pawn shop and a second-hand store sharing the bottom floor. The top three were occupied by families who could manage to scrape together sixty bucks a month for rent out of their welfare checks, after they paid their booze bills. Swan had found his hideaway pad by taking a windowless, single room at the end of the hall in back. I slid my .38 into my hand outside his door and listened to the building. The only sound was the throb of the city outside.

I tried the door slowly, testing the lock, and glanced down the empty hall before I stepped back and kicked hard enough to rip the catch out of the rotting door frames. I wanted Billy to be surprised with his company, but I could have brought a brass band when I went into the room. It was several seconds before the scent registered, and the cold toads started crawling up my back, as I smelled the heavy, close odor of blood. I'd been in too many quiet rooms with dead men not to hear the silent screaming they seem to do. The only thing moving on Billy Swan were the flies.

He was across the bed face up, with his arms outstretched and his head hanging over the edge so that he stared at the door in an upside down fashion, while the flies marched busily over his eyeballs. He wasn't minding that any; they never do when they have a long, red-lipped gash across their throats. He was still dripping some, though the puddle under his head was turning a rusty brown on the edges where it seeped into the bare flooring.

Someone had already talked with Billy Swan, it seemed.

I stood still and listened while I studied the handiwork. You can read a job like a calling card. The gash had been a single vicious stroke that had cut clear through to the spine. The barber's joy, I guessed. A good old-fashioned, straight edge razor job, that had the taste of sadism behind it.

I let my eyes travel the room then, taking in the signs. Someone had made sure Swan wasn't leaving anything behind that could talk when he couldn't. His wallet was stripped, lying on the floor with the contents of his single suitcase. It had been a good search. I didn't bother doing a second one because all I'd had was questions for Swan. There was only the white spot on the leather suitcase that seemed unusual to me. I let the picture kick around in my mind until it clicked that scraping off a travel sticker would leave a mark like that.

That was all that clicked. Someone didn't want anyone to know where Swan had been. I wondered if Luciano was covering his weak spot or if Kincaid had dropped in for a question and answer session that had a one way trip to the black land as a prize at the end of it.

The place was really a dead end.

I took the time to wipe the doorknob clean and found my way back to the car through the alley. I still had the girl, another part of Swan that they would be worried about. I felt my lips pulling tight against my teeth as I headed back to the hotel.

Mistakes are like surprise parties; you make them by thinking you know something that no one else does. I was halfway through the door to my room and was starting to call for Frances when I remembered I shouldn't be that far in at all. I should have been standing in the hall waiting for her to take off the night chain that I'd told her to keep on. Even as I started to turn, I heard the hiss of a sap coming. I knew I was just a little too late, when something made a distant thud against the back of my head.

It was like falling off the world. Seconds inched past like minutes. The sap came back at me out of the dark and slammed against my forehead.

They were being quiet about their work. I made that hard for the one with the sap, because I was reaching as I went down. I wound up with a handful of his crotch. He was choking back a scream when he pounded me over the edge of darkness.

I knew two things as the sounds started creeping into the emptiness. I wasn't quite dead, and I'd been worked by an expert. They had been fast and sure in the pounding. The white shots of pain that kept flashing in my skull meant it was going to get worse. There was a stickiness under my face. I kept lying in it because I didn't think the men in that room wanted me alive one bit.

There are no heroes in my business, and though I may give my all when my life is on the line and take a reasonable amount of risk for the crisp feel of green, I'm not about to get eager when my body won't cooperate with what my mind tells it to do.

I stayed there and listened, with the persistent whimpering of Frances reminding me that I'd brought them the other part of Billy Swan. I'd given them that when I'd tried to put her out of their reach. It only takes seconds for your mind to sort and file those things when your body is limp and almost dead except for pain.

They had left me next to the door. The sounds made me work an eyelid open. That gave me a view of two pairs of shoes pointed toward the dresser next to the bed and a pair of New York casuals which held their owner in front of an easy chair. I guessed he was doing something that added to the leakage under Frances' legs and to the sounds I didn't want to hear.

The guy in the casuals shifted slightly and said, "We're getting nowhere like this. We'll do it my way while we still can."

I forced my eye open more to see Frances and the fun and games they'd had with her until now. I wanted to scream at them because she knew nothing, but Mafia is only sure of that after they dig for their own answers. They dig deep before they stop. I saw the cigarette burn marks on her breasts and a thin line of blood from her ears as one of them pushed her upright in the chair.

"She still hasn't talked."

"She's beyond this. More will only make a shadow out of her. I've seen it."

"No more," Frances said. Her words turned into a whimper.

"Reflex. She don't even know if we're doing anything. Next she goes into shock, and that's it."

"We haven't got anything yet, you ass. Get the stuff. We haven't got all morning." He moved to the bed and picked up a syringe as they talked. I couldn't see higher than their waists. I tried to remember the voices.

"What the hell are you giving her?"

"LSD," the other grunted.

Now sodium pentothal may be an accepted truth serum, especially when you have someone with experience asking the questions, but LSD isn't going to make just anyone a gay flower child, no matter who gives it, if they fight taking a trip. You have to want, really *want*, Utopia to trip out right. When you spend a painful night having questions thrown at you that you can't answer, your mind is ready to welcome a release—even an LSD escape. There was one catch to using the drug though, and that was the chance of a bad trip, where painful reality is a picnic compared to what the mind can deliver. I didn't fancy any of the slobs in the room as experts with more than cigarette butts.

I was right. Twenty minutes after they had given the injection she started screaming. They ended her trip by choking her quietly and leaving her beside me on the floor when they left. I remember hearing the door close before my mind let me slip back into an empty void.

Maybe I'm hard to kill by beating on the head. Maybe they didn't want me dead yet, or Frances' last scream had hurried them into thinking I had enough of my own blood on me to be dead. Whatever it was, I was still doing some dull, pain filled flying later when I started to come around and felt the coolness of sheets over me. It was a reluctant return. Like coming back from where all is quiet and peaceful to big trouble.

"Judas."

I eased open my eyes slowly and realized when the expected pain wasn't there that somewhere along the line a few hypos had been pumped into me. The light hurt when I opened both eyes, but I kept them open until the features of Butcher swam into focus.

"Glad to see you made the party, Red," I said. "Where in hell am I?"

"County Hospital downtown," he said. "But go soft on the talk. The doc said I could wait if I kept you quiet."

"I don't feel talkative anyway."

Some intern must have been working on his merit badge for knot tying, because my head felt like the latest thing in turbans. I touched the bandages, looked at Butcher and knew there was some bad news coming when I said, "I don't suppose all of this is a state secret, so give. What happened?"

He shoved a cigarette between his lips before he started. "I walked in on the whole mess, you and the girl. I knew I couldn't cover that so I lifted your .38 and rig and called a homicide detective I knew. He's in the hall now, but he doesn't expect to get much from you." He paused, then said, "The guy's okay, Judas."

"Aren't they all?" I said. "When do I get out of here?"

He shrugged. "A few days, maybe."

I tried to grin at him. "Not while I got a contract running, it's no three days, Red. We pull some strings now maybe—Cardinalli's strings."

"It figures," he said. "You've been in here since this morning, and someone's already put that Ford of yours in the lot outside. Maybe they want you out and working where they can get at you." His face was set in a mask that I couldn't read. "What's the matter? In a hurry to get to your own funeral?"

I let my eyes focus on the pale green of the far wall. Its blankness was something a guy could use to relax and get lost in. I kept myself from drifting away by reaching for my smokes on the night stand.

"Not my funeral," I told him. "I'm in a hurry to arrange for a few wakes, though. I was there before the girl died, Red. And don't hand me any crap about your pal outside and the police. I've got a private grudge to settle now too. It's my head they worked on."

He didn't answer me for a moment. Then he said quietly, "I figured it like that. That's why I called Thierney in. Your stuff will be at the bar when you get out, and I left another suit in the closet there."

I glanced at the hospital gown I was wearing and said, "White never was my color."

He mashed out his cigarette and looked at me some more. "Want to fill me in on it?"

I shrugged. "Billy Swan, the girl, both leads to where they're keeping the kid, I'd guess. All you can do now is keep an ear open for another lead. Get everything you can about Luciano now."

"It could get you more trouble, Judas."

I touched my head and flinched. "You mean there's more trouble than what I've got now?"

He tossed me a lopsided grin and picked up his hat. "I'll try," he said. "One thing though, Detective Thierney owed me a favor when I called him, so you're logged in here as an accident victim. He's going to try like hell to get more on this, but he knows how Mafia works too. You get what I mean?"

I watched him go to the door and thanked his hate for being able to pull a few strings too. "I only hope Thierney understands how I work," I told him as he went out. "I hope that it's good and clear to him."

CHAPTER FIVE

Detective Thierney didn't surprise me. He was an old cop, and while I wasn't a backer of cops, I'd met a few in the past that I'd respected. I knew that the profession tended to mold the character of the man following it. Thierney's years as a cop, with so many bodies, so many unsolved squeals, might have pushed home the fact that most of his rules were dreams, and he had to play it by ear. He'd also been around enough to know about an inter-racket gun like me to figure that maybe my gun was pointed at the people he couldn't touch. He didn't need to like it. All he had to do was avoid making a major case out of it.

I studied him when he came into the room. He was a small, thin man with a bald head and eyes that seemed dead tired. He looked typecast for a part that said he should own a mortgaged house and have a family in the suburbs—like three kids and a wife who worried about his winding up on a slab at the ice house.

Thierney helped himself to a seat beside the bed, took

out a dog-eared notebook and said, "You're a public charge right now, mister. I hope you're carrying enough to pick up this tab and some paper work which didn't come cheap."

"I'll pick it up. I didn't expect favors."

"What happened at the hotel?"

"What hotel? All I know is that I had an accident. Maybe I got rolled."

Thierney frowned and went on like he didn't hear me. "Not the girl too, mister. When Cardinalli's and Luciano's names start coming up, I like to know why. It doesn't matter if I'm doing favors or not."

"Maybe they don't like each other. How's that sound?"

He studied me a moment, then said, "I saw the girl too, Jones. I've worked at these things long enough to know it's a murder I'd like to solve without seeing you again, too."

"Sure," I said. "So now, tell me all about the convictions you get on this sort of a kill." I shrugged. "Anyway, you've come this far with it, and I'm not in the Cook County slammer."

"For Butcher, I went this far," he said. "Now I hope it was worth it or I could change my mind."

"What would make it worth your trouble?"

He didn't like the way I'd said that. I watched the play of distaste cross his face, like something was chewing at his guts. He folded his notebook carefully, and his face went blank again. "You're playing on your own team," he said flatly. "And you're lucky to be alive right now. Why or how you work doesn't matter to me, but Butcher does, and he gave me the idea that you'd be interested in who killed the girl, too."

I studied the wall. "If there was a girl in my 'accident,' she was a ten buck whore, and I wouldn't owe her a thing, would I?"

My words didn't change his expression any. "She might have been that," he said. "If she was, she still knew something that Cardinalli or Luciano wanted. I'd like to hang it on them. I'd like to see the ones who hire slobs like you pay for just one of these. It happens to be my job."

He knew how to stir up the sourness that had been in my guts since I'd seen the flies walking across Billy Swan's eyeballs. I kept remembering the fear in Frances' eyes, because she knew there was nothing she could tell them. The thoughts were on the thin edge of my voice when I said, "Yeah, and you know like Butcher does that you're lousy at your job when it comes to Mafia. Only Butcher went and played it their way once. They understood that."

"Like you play it, I suppose?"

I didn't answer that one.

Thierney seemed to be picking his words as he went on. "Like I told you, you're on the books here as an accident. If you're really careful, you might get a chance to walk out of here and have another one." He waited patiently for a moment. "I can wait until one of you makes a mistake, and then maybe I'll have a body to hang on someone."

"That's lousy police procedure."

"Murder and people like you are lousy business," he said. "Butcher thinks you might want some information on our local talent. Do you?"

"Did he think of a price for the information, too?"

His face went tight for a moment. Then, watching me he said, "I'm glad I don't have to like you, Jones. You've got a personality that would make it a pleasure to slam a steel door on." He paused a moment. "My information isn't for sale, and in case that's a rare thing to you, I'll tell you why. I get my pay and kicks by hanging around to see you people kill each other off. So, is there any particular information you want?"

I made myself grin and I got a cigarette going, while I felt the pounding inside my head pick up with the movement. "Nice attitude you've got," I said. "Only, let's say you're still too damn helpful for a cop. Let me in on the catch."

"Butcher's the catch," he said, finally. "He doesn't tell me how far he'll go now for a chance to screw up anything Mafia. I don't ask him either, but since I'm his friend, I don't want to see him turn up on a slab at the morgue."

"My turning up there wouldn't matter. Is that it?"

"He's a friend," he shrugged. "You bought yourself that one-way ticket to a slab a long time ago, anyway."

"No one's collected it yet, cop," I said. "Not quite yet."

"That's how it is, though. The catch with Butcher is like this. You keep him out of any heavy stuff, and I'm helpful with information."

I let him wait a moment before I nodded. "He's not in anything but leg work."

"Good. Keep it like that by remembering that if he has an 'accident' in this, there won't be a hole you can hide your ass in. I mean it, Jones."

I looked at his eyes and didn't doubt him a bit.

"Now, let's hear the questions," he said.

I shook my head which only managed to stir up the pounding some more, while I dug around for some missing answers I needed. There were some real nice ones I couldn't ask, so I settled for, "All right, this isn't my city, and I'm running on grapevine. Give me a rundown on how the rackets look by your files."

"Big order," he said flatly. "But Cardinalli, Luciano and Nicholas Pappas are the ones who pull the strings now."

"How does Pappas fit? Just one of Cardinalli's boys, or more?"

Thierney didn't spend much time on the question. He shifted his cigarette around in his mouth and talked like he was reading a police report.

"He's one of the boys, but a big one, maybe next in line after Cardinalli. I don't think he'd make a move without Cardinalli's O.K., though. He's right up there where he could pressure his boss if he wanted to. We figure him for the one who does the real planning behind a party like you attended—all with Cardinalli's approval. How's that fit?"

"Lousy," I said. "How about Luciano?"

"Yeah, the city's 'Boy Wonder.' A perfect example of the hood sure to succeed or get dead fast. He's been a surprise to us for some time now. You figure it out—a small time punk chewing at the racket's edge and likely to stay like that. But then, the surprise comes in, and he gets brave enough to start pushing. It was close to two years ago that our stoolies started feeding us information, that Luciano was getting brave enough to take some big bites out of Cardinalli's action."

"Maybe he just got tired of living, huh?"

Thierney pushed the crack aside and went on. "Who knows for sure what a punk like that gets on his mind? I've watched this one happen. There's a pattern to every grab he's made so far. They all have worked, Jones. Like maybe someone is leaking out Cardinalli's business to him. I can't see Luciano always being 'Lucky Punk on the Spot,' who just happens to have his boys ready to move in where Cardinalli isn't ready to stop him. That much luck would be real funny, wouldn't it?"

"Yeah, I'll laugh myself to death about it," I told him. "From what I hear, Cardinalli is going to stop him now."

"Uh huh," Thierney nodded. "But, it's not going to be as easy as stepping on a bug any more. Luciano, to us, is big enough to be a real problem now. Cardinalli can't start on him without expecting to get a dose of police heat too, and he knows that it can't be an old fashioned gang war." He paused and let me think about that. "Let's put it like this; Luciano is big enough to have a few strings to pull. He's right where even we don't go after him without an okay and a push from the D.A."

"Nice," I said. "Has the D.A. been doing any pushing lately?"

He grinned at me and meant it for the first time as he said, "Let's just say that he's interested enough right now to collect a little information and do some fishing. And you, mister, are one of the baited hooks we have now. We'll sit back and wait until something bites." He sat there, looking like he could wait out a rock, sure of himself behind the tired eyes. He knew I didn't have the time to wait.

"Nice game you're playing, isn't it?" I asked. "No matter how it comes out, you figure the public will benefit."

His smile stayed fixed. "That's right," he admitted easily. "Anyway it goes now, we'll get one or two of you people out of our hair. You people taught us how to play the game. I'll use you to get at Cardinalli or Luciano, just like you're using Butcher and maybe used that girl. You might even think you're using me now, but I can pull some strings too, can't I?"

I kept watching his smile.

"And when it's over," he went on, "don't let me catch you near any bodies. Don't leave any of those around at all or you're all mine." He put his cigarette out and reached for his hat. "We understand each other pretty well now, don't we?"

I turned my head to watch him as he put on his hat. His face didn't tell me a thing except that he meant every bit of it, and I knew he'd play it exactly like he said.

"We understand each other fine," I said. "So, I'll look behind me if I explore any dark alleys."

A laugh got out around his grin. "I won't be that close, Jones, so save yourself the trouble. I'll just be there waiting to see who takes the bait."

"Nobody will be doing anything until I'm out of

here. How do I work that? Just get up and walk out, maybe?"

"Check out and pay your bill like a good citizen, might be a better idea. There won't be any police around to stop you!" He walked as far as the door and turned. "But that's no guarantee that *someone* won't be waiting, is it? You're a nice target now, Judas," he added quietly.

I watched the door click shut behind him and closed my eyes against the pounding in my head. The one thing I knew about Thierney was that he was right, and I knew where part of the stink was coming from on this contract because he'd told me that too. I went off to sleep not liking the idea of being bait for a cop who could wait. It made me wonder when Cardinalli would be sending someone around to check on the bait he had hired.

It was dark outside the room when I came back to the land of the living for a second time. The protective edge of unconsciousness peeled away from me slowly. I got a re-run of the girl's screaming inside my mind. It was like coming out of a booze sleep, filled with bad dreams, until the darkness snapped away abruptly because you realized that the screaming had been real. I wanted to crawl back into the darkness and let reality go away again, until the sound of a cigarette lighter and someone's breathing registered to me. It took me a few seconds to get an eyelid open to look and then wish I hadn't.

With a smile and a patient look, Kincaid was sitting next to the bed. It was like waking up and finding a fed snake in bed with you. I was getting damned tired of patient people.

"What the hell do you want?" I asked, almost closing my eyes over the throb that followed the words through my skull.

"I'm checking on the number one patsy for today,"

he said. "The boss is funny like that. He likes to keep track of his investments. You walked into that head whipping like a virgin, I suppose?"

"You could have done better, maybe? I didn't expect Luciano to know more about this job than I did, that's for sure. So tell Cardinalli that someone is due a busted mouth because I got a busted head. Someone talked."

He shrugged it off. "You just got a big bump, not a busted skull. In fact, the doc says there's nothing busted on you at all. Whoever did you up must do sloppy work."

"Maybe they wanted me around for seconds. I don't suppose you have any idea who they were?"

His grin tightened some. "You've been doing such a nice job of making sure you lose me that I didn't get there to see who did the work. All I saw around was cops, and I drifted away from that."

"Why don't you do some drifting now? Go back and kiss Pappas' ass or something to keep in practice and tell Cardinalli I'm still on this. Nothing's changed."

"I got some words of wisdom for you," he said softly, "a message. You ain't going to have any job at all if you don't get back on it fast. The boss doesn't pay any sick leave for this, and he's worried about the kid."

I closed my eyes and listened to him get up.

"Call tomorrow and make the boss happy that you're working," Kincaid said. "You do that, or you'll make me happy with a job, and the boss will make you real unpopular around town."

I watched the play of pleasure on his face while he thought about that. Then he left. I spent a long time watching the door after he was gone. The night gave me time to think out the pieces I had. A gray, false dawn with rain had appeared before I gave it up as a lot of parts that didn't match or make sense. What came nearest to fitting was the idea Butcher had started and Thierney's talk had added to. I'd been hired to fill in a spot for something more than finding the girl. If I accepted that, it followed that I hadn't started the looking and maybe wasn't scheduled to end it. I didn't care for the way that added up at all, so I tucked the idea away, because I wasn't going to forget it. I decided that it would be nice to know what Cardinalli was playing for besides his daughter's life.

There was no more sleep for me in the lame end of the morning. I used the time to talk a nurse into finding me a razor and letting me shower and shave. She didn't like it, but a paying guest is always right. I guessed that Thierney had pulled one of his strings and impressed the doctor with his badge.

I was dressed and waiting when the doctor came into the room. He watched me while I pointed to the gauze wrapping on my head and asked, "Does anything fall apart if you take that off?"

He took it off and poked and prodded, and he watched my lips twitch while he shined his light into my eyes. He grunted finally and said, "You've taken quite a blow to the head. There can still be complications. I advise another day in bed."

"There already are complications from that blow, doc," I said. "But no more bed. Check me out of here."

He wore an expression that said someone hadn't left him much choice, and it must have been a sharp dig to his professional mind. He kept shaking his head as he led me to the desk and signed my release papers.

I found the cashier in the lobby downstairs and used some of Cardinalli's money to pay the bill. When I walked out into the light rain, I remembered the rented Ford that Butcher had said was in the parking lot. In spite of the headache I managed to grin. They're real nice, the people I work for. They wanted me out and moving. They couldn't be sure if I had learned anything or not, but it was important to them that I was active.

I kept thinking like that until I found the Ford and slid in behind the wheel. It took me a few minutes to find the keys tucked in back of the sun visor. Maybe it was people being so overly helpful that made me stop before I used the ignition. It made me wonder suddenly just *who* had been so kind to bring the car over. Butcher hadn't. He'd only seen it here. That left too many people, who didn't like me, that could have been helpful.

I put the keys down on the seat and felt the sweat start to crawl down my face. Then I lay down on the seat and took a look under the dash. It was there all right. The ideal way for my helpful friends to help me out—right out of the world! I counted the five dirty yellow sticks taped to the steering wheel column and traced two thin wires leading to the ignition. It wasn't an elaborate job, just a nice, simple piece of work by someone who had known what he was doing. It looked real effective. All there would have been was one big flash and a lot of wide awake patients in the hospital if I had turned the key on.

I sat there and let myself shake some before I wiped my hands and checked a cute second fuse that might have been hooked to the break pedal. Then I cut the wires next to the ignition with my fingernail clippers and lifted the sticks out easily. I've got a healthy respect for dynamite when it's delivered like that.

I sweated some more while I remembered how many ways there are to booby trap a car. The charge I had on the seat could be just a decoy. The real charge could be a very cute arrangement some place else and set to smear me over a city block.

Even if it did figure that Luciano wouldn't try anything fancy when a simple way would do it, it wasn't a chance I wanted to take. I pulled my jacket off and checked the whole assembly like I was going to put a charge in the car myself, while the doctors and interns stared curiously at me as they passed by on their way to work. It would have been easy to walk off and leave the car for the poor slob who'd be around to haul it off in time. Only, their job didn't include murder, and mine did. While I sweated over the checking, I wanted Luciano to know that his bug bang hadn't worked either.

Later I put the five sticks into the trunk and held my breath as I started the car. I listened to the growl of the motor and felt the tension ease when I nosed into the morning traffic for a run over to Butcher's place.

There wasn't any tail that I could spot on the way over. I parked in front of the bar and felt hate chewing at my guts, like Butcher must feel every time he looked in a mirror to shave. I knew I shouldn't let my own feelings push me into making any mistakes. I was good at holding back, but there was enough getting through to give me an idea how easy it would be to muff it. You can feel that hate creeping around inside you like acid.

Butcher was sleepy-eyed behind the bar. He fed me good booze while he listened to the morning's events. Finally he slid my shoulder rig and .38 over the bar. His mouth was too tight and the eyes too cold as he watched me strap it on and pull my jacket over it. He wasn't trying to make them that way. They just were. Like an old cop watching a young hood who hasn't quite gone over the line yet.

I settled down with the feel of iron under my arm again and took a pull at my cigarette while I watched his eyes.

"Let's hear it, if you've got anything, Red. Billy Swan and the girl are dead ends now, and we don't need to argue about someone wanting me out of this for good after the events of this morning."

He found a glass to polish, and you could see him peeling back the years in his mind, until the cop part of him was there and he was trying to put together a case. He was a past expert at Mafia and tailor-made misery when he dug for a weak spot to let his hate in where it would hurt.

Watching it happen in his face, I realized that I wasn't at all sure about the risks he was willing to take with me out front to get his swing at the rackets. He returned my gaze during his thoughts, looking as though he were judging two dogs which were going to fight.

"They know Swan didn't give you anything, not even a good guess where he'd been," he said. "They must still think that his girl could have. So, they can't let up and take the chance. It could explain the set-up in the car this morning."

"We still only have dead ends. No matter what they think. I hope the bastards get ulcers worrying about it though."

"There's an odd part about the Swan killing, too. It's a little bit out of line to scrape a decal off a suitcase. Don't you think? Unless it was something they didn't want you to know about—some place maybe. If it had been a city decal they wouldn't have bothered because you still wouldn't know where to start."

"Okay," I said. "Go ahead and play cop. There's a hell of a lot of places to get decals, you know, and I don't have a place to start looking at the moment."

He smiled with the scar and picked up another glass to work on. "We can eliminate a lot of places for that decal to have come from. Just figure it like this: how many places would a hood like Swan visit? Only a place where he'd have his own type of company is a fair guess."

The early morning booze was working on me fast. I felt the pain behind my eyes ease some. I said, "Okay, so we're likely right to figure that Swan wasn't the travel for fun type, and he didn't get vacations unless Luciano sent him some place to cool off. That would fit Swan pretty good, I'd say."

Butcher didn't seem to do anything but dig deeper in his mind. He nodded absently and went on with his glass polishing.

"It's a long shot," he said. "But I wonder what sort

of place Luciano might have to send his boys for a rest. A resort area maybe?"

I let the idea trickle through my mind and picked up what he was getting at. A long shot like he'd said, but a calculated one. Swan had been out of town lately, and he'd evidently been to the same place before, or he wouldn't have had a decal on his bags. It made sense why the decal had been scraped off if it advertised a place the girl could be kept. This was a thin straw to clutch, I know, but it had the quality of being the only straw in sight.

"Nice bunch of ifs and maybes there," I said. "How would we go about finding Luciano's little hideaway, if there even is one?"

Butcher put the second glass down and poured me another drink. "It could be interesting to run a check on the property he owns."

I shook my head. "We haven't got the time to check it."

"Let me call Thierney," Butcher said. "They might have what we want right there, since they're interested in Luciano too. They've already had time to do the checking."

"I don't like owing your friend any favors, when he's waiting for nothing more than a chance to drop an ax on me." I spit the words out.

Butcher looked thoughtful. "It's the same ax for the others too. Be smart and don't be there when it falls."

"Yeah. He gave me that bit of advice, too," I said. "Everybody is waiting for a mistake to get made. I don't want to be the one who makes it. I've got a feeling it would be fatal."

It was hard to guess what Butcher was thinking. His eyes had a trick of going blank like mirrors that didn't work. I wondered if I was using him or if he was judging how far he could use me. I kept thinking that he hadn't come into this for money. It was supposed to make me feel better, but I kept remembering that even money couldn't wipe out what he felt.

He brought it out nice and slow after a while with "You came to me with this, Judas. Now you can play it like it falls from Thierney or say the word and I'll get out too. I'm telling you it's a chance. Do we use it or not?"

I hid behind the drink for a moment and watched him over the rim of the glass. "I don't like favors from cops," I told him. "We don't exactly have the same interests in mind."

"I'll be asking for the favor," Butcher said. "Well?"

"Go ahead," I shrugged. "Call him. I'm going to take a drive out to Swan's cabin on the lake. He might have another suitcase there. One decal and we'll know if we're in business or not."

He smiled in a dead way, and I could see his eyes fix on the spot where my .38 sat. "Don't forget Bello and Potts either, Judas. If Luciano doesn't hear the big bang he had planned for this morning, you can bet he'll put them back out looking for you."

I stopped at the door and nodded at him. It would be a little hard to forget the two who would get paid for making me into a corpse. You don't forget them when you know they're pros who won't quit. You also remembered that it was their own backyard, and that left you few choices. You ran, or you let them catch you where you wanted them to.

"One more thing, Butcher," I said. "Has either Potts or Bello got a reputation as a bomb man?"

"I wondered when you'd get around to that," he said and nodded. "Frankie Bello has. I hear that he's a juice man from a long time ago. Maybe he likes the sound when one of his bombs goes off."

I didn't think Butcher's crack was funny. The rain outside seemed to pull the clouds down on the tops of the building. I could feel the weather's damp chill against my face as I drove toward the lake and thought about Luciano's little helpers.

It was close to noon now, and it might be a few hours before Luciano sent Potts and Bello back out. I hoped that they were local talent and that they would worry some when they found out the bomb hadn't worked. It might make them listen to the rumors they'd be hearing. It would give them something to think about until I got back to the city and found them first.

I pushed the thought aside and got the Ford onto Outer Drive, heading north until I found the blacktop cut off above Highland Park. I drove toward the lake. I checked for a tail right along, and by the time the lake lay before me, I knew I hadn't brought anyone with me.

It took me close to an hour before I found the right dirt cut off to Billy Swan's cottage. The place was a small, one floor building that sat in a clump of wind-twisted pines, about fifty yards from the beach. I left the car in the pines, out of sight, and walked in. The waves and rain covered the sound of the glass I broke from the window on the rear porch. I watched the beach for a while before I pulled the catch and eased it up.

Inside it was cool and damp, with the overcast turning the rooms into a gray darkness. I slid the .38 into my hand and walked to the front of the cottage, making a quick check of the rooms. The musty odor told me Swan hadn't used the place lately. At least they didn't seem to have used the place to keep the girl, but I hadn't figured on getting that lucky with my visit. In fact, I thought all I was going to get was a little exercise from the morning's work. I searched the bedroom and found no sign of luggage.

Then I found the photo album in the dresser and glanced through it. The first photos of Sandy Cardinalli were halfway through the book. It took me a moment to dig out the photo Cardinalli had given me. The face was the same when I matched them up with the pictures in the album. I studied the faces of her companions and tried to juggle it into some sense. There wasn't any doubt left about Swan having known her long before the time he helped pull off the snatch—a fact that could mean exactly nothing or everything if I ran into any of the other men in the photos. I knew one more face besides Sandy's and Swan's, and I pulled that photo out for possible later use. It wasn't because the man had his arm around Sandy in a way that was a little more than friendship. I kept that photo because I had an idea it was the key to when this job really started, and that was long before I took the contract. As Butcher said, it looked like I'd been dropped into a mess as a fill in. It made me wonder if anyone had me scheduled to finish the job. I shook my head and kept flipping album pages, because I was guessing and grabbing at straws. There could be some logical answers for Sandy to turn up in Swan's album. If there was a legitimate answer for it, I was right back at the start again.

Finishing the search of the cottage gave me a big nothing to add to the photos. There wasn't a hint of a lead that would take me any place else Swan had been. The dead end made by cutting his throat was as empty as the wind sounded outside. I smiled tightly to myself and went back out through the window, with a hope that Butcher was having better luck, because there wasn't any time left to play on long shots. It had to be soon, or it wasn't going to be at all.

It was nearly dark when I got back to the city and started a bit of bar hopping in Luciano's territory—only to see if he had his disciples back out hunting. I hoped they were.

CHAPTER SIX

The light rain kept the sidewalks empty on Maxwell Street. As I walked along shadows cast by neon lights were my only company. In that neighborhood, the bars were close enough for me to leave the Ford parked in one spot. I knew the area was Luciano's playground, but even so, it took me three hours before I started getting a reaction. I caught fish-eyed looks and listened to the whispers. I began to get treated like I had a bad case of B.O. I knew who I was looking for from Butcher's description. I knew, too, that every bar was equipped with a creep who had a spare dime in his pocket and an urge to please Luciano by spreading the word.

In two places, the bartender gave me a negative shake of the head. In a dive on the corner of the block, the bartender pushed a drink at me before he began to wipe the bar a few feet away. There was sweat growing on his face while he studied me out of the corner of his eye and glanced at the door. Whatever he was thinking, he didn't look like he was going to put any heavy money on my future.

He came back over when I held my glass up and asked, "Freshen it up, will you? And this time try to get some whisky in it."

He chewed on his lower lip as he brought the drink back. He kept his hand on the glass until I looked up at him. Then he said, "Mac, if you don't like the drinks here, why don't you try Sal's Bar up the street. I hear they hand out some good set-ups there."

His head bobbed slightly when he said "set-up," and he rolled his eyes like it was a dirty word. It wasn't hard to read his face. The fear that guys like Bello and Potts live on was there. It didn't take too much thought to get the drift of what he was saying.

You don't sit in a place and ask a man why he's passing on a tip like that, when it could be anything. Like maybe he didn't dig Luciano's hand in his cash register every week, or maybe something as simple as not liking either Potts' or Bello's looks. Whatever it was, you didn't shake his hand for the tip. You didn't say thanks either, if you wanted to see him go on living. So I just looked at him and let my lips twist into a smirk before I picked up the drink and tasted it.

I looked at the glass in disgust as I set it down. "Yeah, if this is the kind of slop you push, slob, maybe I will try another bar."

"Do that," he said. "And let's have a buck and a half for your drink first."

I tipped my glass over and watched it splash across the bar. "That crap's not worth a buck even." I tossed a crumpled ten spot on the bar while I got off the stool. "You're getting overpaid with that."

He had the ten in his pocket and was swearing at me when I left.

Sal's Bar was a half block up the street. While I walked toward the place, I could feel everything in me tightening up like someone was winding my guts on a fork. I didn't like it working out with me not picking the place, but they were pros and had played it cute by staying ahead of me until they were sure I was looking. Now they were ready to let me find them.

There were some ways around it, I knew. I could avoid it and wait for a better time, but they would only use that time as a chance to play it safer—like planting some more bombs, and I don't enjoy walking on eggs. I thought about Bello and his helpful little packages, and I knew that he wouldn't attempt a simple plant on the second try.

I found a way around to the back of Sal's Bar and walked in through the garbage route. The rear hall was dark and filled with the smell of old booze and the sound of the juke box. The music grew louder when I eased the door to the bar open a crack and took a look at my reception party.

You had to admit that they did good work. It was set up nice—only not quite nice enough, because they kept doing it the easy way, like they were forgetting I made a living at it too. Thinking like that had put Bello at my end of the room at a table with his back to me. He could watch Potts, who was at the bar and doing a detail study of the bar mirror which gave him a full view of the front door. The rest of the customers were hard at the process of getting drunk and couldn't have cared less about the two slow drinkers.

While I eased a knife out of my jacket and let the thin blade whisper against my hand, I wondered what Bello had on his mind. I knew damn well he wasn't thinking about what he was going to get. I waited until he picked up his glass before I went inside and stepped up behind him.

There wasn't anything I had to tell Bello about his bomb habits, but in that fraction of a second, when he felt my hand on his shoulder and the blade as it slid in high between his ribs, he had time to think over why he was dead. I felt him try to get up under my hand before he sagged back onto the table like a drunk. I moved halfway across the room, with the knife up against my sleeve. It was about a three second trip, one that seemed to take me a week to make, but it was worth it because Potts blinked stupidly at my reflection behind him and let his mouth fall open slowly like a fish.

"Guess what, punk," I said. "Now you found me."

Potts knew things weren't happening as planned, and it might have been fun to watch him sweat and wonder why. Only that would let the confusion settle some in his head, and you didn't give a pro that. I gave Potts all I was going to give him when I pulled him around and dragged the blade across just above his belt.

The bartender was looking at us then. Potts looked like he was trying to hold a butcher shop inside his shirt. I turned away and kept on walking.

I was almost out the door before someone noticed Potts was having stomach problems and started screaming. A moment later I was outside in the rain, thinking it would take a lot of sewing thread and loving care to put Potts back together. He was just as messy as I wanted him. Bello wasn't messy, he was just dead. Between the two of them Luciano's gang should get the point that a dirty hand can be played by anyone in the game.

It was close to eleven before I got back to the Ford and pointed it towards the Loop area. There was one more stop to make before the night was over. I felt the sweat creeping down my back and a chill in my guts as I let the traffic pull me across the city's face. The cigarette I lit danced around the shaking light. I was used to the feeling because it always followed a thing like Potts and Bello. Each job brings a sense of sickness with it, like death riding my shoulders for a while. Just a reminder that the next time it could be me who was leaking his guts out into some gutter.

But not yet, I told myself. Not this time. Tonight it

would be my work on the grapevine, and they would remember, because a sharp piece of cold steel makes even a racket man's ass pucker up. It's not at all like standing back with a .38. It would make them less eager about finding me, and I needed everything I could get on my side.

Watching the rain outside wrap a misty grayness around the city, I pushed Maxwell Street out of my mind. It gets easier to do that after being in the racket a few years—maybe because you know your circle is a closed one and sooner or later everyone gets what Potts and Bello got. You know, too, that a kill is easier to forget when you are also handing fear back to some of the Mafia.

I kept the Ford with the traffic and hoped that a lot of Luciano's people wouldn't like the news on the grapevine tomorrow. It would bother them knowing I was right at home and could play it just as dirty as they could. A few surprises like that could make Luciano spooky, like finding out that for once everyone was getting a chance at being the target.

I grinned to myself. I had always liked bringing surprises around anyway—even when they made me the hottest son of a bitch in the city, and that's what I figured I was going to be as soon as Luciano got the news about his pride and joy pair of butcher boys tonight.

Just as I knew that I'd be on the top of Luciano's "things to take care of" list tomorrow, I also knew that it would be a three-sided affair from now on: Luciano, Cardinalli's contract which seemed to include more than his daughter, and Thierney, the cop who was willing to collect a pound of flesh for society no matter who won. It was three-sided trouble any way you looked at it. All I needed now was for Kincaid to decide to start doing his job and to stick close, like he would when the finish came.

I thought about Kincaid some, then about Maxwell

Street and decided that the night needed one more thing. I found a liquor store and picked up a bottle before I checked into a unit in the rear of a motel. I could have told myself that I was being careful by staying off some hot streets, but I didn't need to lie to myself. I was going to get carefully drunk, and I was going to get that way as quickly as whisky could do it. It made sense to be hard to find while I did it.

An hour of careful attention to the bottle got me blind enough to flop on the bed but not far enough out to stop my thinking. I wanted to call Butcher and tell him to come up with something fast because the job had me on the wall, and there was no place to go now. I needed another thread to follow that might take me to Luciano's daughter.

You could hate Luciano's guts, but you had to give him one thing. He didn't leave any leads lying around except dead ones. And after tonight, he wouldn't care about what I knew; he would just want me dead. He was caught in a bind too, playing his big gamble now, and somehow he wanted to continue to play until he had Cardinalli's answer before he finally moved. Unless Luciano was taking stupid pills, he was waiting for an answer to a question he already knew. There didn't seem to be any logical thinking behind that sort of move.

My own boozed up logic wasn't so hot along those lines either. Cardinalli kept crowding the booze in my mind with random thoughts. Pappas and Kincaid seemed to hold the keys to the rest of the contract. I had the middle of it, but it seemed that both ends were still open and waiting for some answers.

I let it drift through my mind from the beginning and couldn't come up with a kidnap pattern or any other pattern that would fit what I knew so far. I couldn't see Luciano eating his way up the dung heap bit by bit and then calmly making himself a target that Cardinalli had to go after. The Lucianos of the rackets do not get that brave or stupid no matter how they feel.

Still trying to sort it out, I fell asleep. The sound of the rain outside helped to keep me sleeping until late into the morning. When I finally made my eyes stay open at ten and took a shower, I had the sour taste of booze in my mouth and a guilty knowledge of time running out.

Cardinalli was at his office-apartment and didn't look the least bit pleased to see me. His watchdogs were absent at the moment, and I took time to study the man as I sat across from him, with my hat in my lap. It wasn't that his business-like, dignified appearance surprised me, like it would the people who typecast all Mafia as slobs, equipped with stingy brim hats and sunglasses. It was just that I had some interesting questions to ask, and I wanted to see if there was going to be any twitching done by the fatherly figure when he gave the answers.

He hid his opinion of my presence by absorbing himself in trimming and lighting a cigar. Finally he let out his dislike by blowing smoke at me as he said. "You should know better than to come here, Jones. What in hell is so important?"

"I've got a little problem. There are too damn many people trying to kill me. That just doesn't add up right, when our little deal was so hush, hush. Our friend, Luciano, has known all along I'm in on this. Now why in hell is that?"

He looked at me for a little while and toyed with his cigar. "These things get around. Hell, maybe they had a man watching you when we picked you up. You know there is a risk on a contract."

"Better yet, maybe someone with a big mouth is a good answer. I'm not wild about being put on anyone's kill list, Cardinalli. I don't like games played with me either. I put one in the morgue and one in the hospital last night over this, so don't be cute about anything."

"You got a big dislike for me fast, Judas," he said, and watched me curiously. "It shows, but maybe you dislike everyone you work for, huh?"

"What counts is that I like their money. I don't even mind the work I do for that. It's the cute little games I worry about, because they can get me killed without knowing why, and I'd hate to die curious."

"Games?"

I nodded. "Odd little things, like why is this job putting me one step behind everyone else? You wouldn't be laying off your bets by having someone out looking for the kid besides me, would you?"

"No one's out," he said. "My boys are sitting tight and don't like it. We asked a few questions around, before you took it, and that's all. It's just you and Kincaid."

"And he's supposed to be just watching me, right?" I asked. "I'm getting the idea I'm last man in line from the bodies I keep walking into and can't talk to."

"Luciano's out there," he reminded me. "No one from here. Kincaid watches and keeps you both careful. Do you think I want this job screwed up?"

"It's too bad, if you don't, because it *is* screwed up, Cardinalli, and my being careful doesn't help a bit when Luciano does a better job of it."

He put down his cigar and let the smile get away from him while he stared at me across his desk. "What's your point?"

"I'm missing somewhere. Run this snatch job down to me again and don't leave anything out this time."

"You got all of that."

"Not *all* of it, Cardinalli. You want your kid back. I want it too. If the cute playing doesn't stop, it might not work out that way."

There aren't too many people around Cardinalli who don't agree with him on cue. It was a new experience that made him let a full minute pass before he shook his head and hid behind the cigar again. "You've heard everything I know about this."

And that was it. I couldn't shake him from the statement. He sat behind his cigar and wore a bland expression that didn't match his eyes. Finally I grinned at him and said, "Then I'll give *you* some news, Cardinalli."

There were a few quiet moments that he used to stare at me coldly before he shrugged, "I doubt if there is much you can tell me about this or my daughter."

It was my turn to shrug. "How close were you to your daughter, Cardinalli? Did you really know what made her tick?"

"You'd better explain that," he said, and for a moment the anger got to his face.

"Like, did you know any of the people she ran around with? Her crowd, you could call it."

"She was old enough to choose her own friends. I didn't involve myself with that part of her life."

"How about her male friends? She bring them around for an okay from you?"

"I wasn't asked to pass any judgment on those either," he informed me. "She had enough male friends too, if that's what you mean."

I kept my eyes on him as I pulled the picture of Sandy and Billy Swan from my pocket and pushed it over the desk in front of him.

"That's her and a friend, isn't it, Cardinalli?"

He picked up the picture carefully and worked on his cigar while anger returned to his eyes. "Where did you get this?"

"It seems that Luciano's man, Billy Swan, kept a picture album of past events," I said. "It must have made it a lot easier later when the snatch came around. He just went out and put the grab on an old friend." I waited a moment. "You knew Swan when you looked at the picture, but you never mentioned this little friendship before and the Luciano connection. Is that a private bit of dirty family laundry or something?"

Cardinalli tossed the picture back toward me. "I didn't dig into her private life, damn it! This is the first I knew of her even knowing Swan. How can I tell you what I don't know?"

I took the picture back and pulled another from my pocket, holding it while I studied his face. "How long have you and Sandy been at not liking each other? Did she walk out of here to shack up with someone, Cardinalli?"

"Judas," he said quietly, "you're running at the mouth to hear the wind in your ears. Can you see a young girl walking out on what she had?"

"The truth? Yes," I nodded. "It's a good question though. Why in hell would she leave?" I smiled. "Unless she thought she had something better going. How does that hit you?"

He didn't move right away, like he was asking himself how much I'd take. Or maybe it took a few seconds for what I kept hinting at to get through because it just wasn't done. There is nothing more goddamn sensitive than a big crook who lives respectably as a second act. You know that, and you don't hint at any dirt on a man's daughter, unless you are trying to get a reaction. Cardinalli didn't look polite when he came around the desk. He was either an excellent actor or he was dead serious. There wasn't any doubt that the back-handed slap he chopped across my face was real.

I saw it coming and took it, feeling his ring cut into my cheek. He had that one coming, if I was wrong. But I caught his wrist when he tried for seconds and smiled at him while a thin line of blood crept down my cheek. I said, "One is all you get for free, Cardinalli. Go back and sit down."

"Punk!" he said. "No punk puts his mouth on my blood like that. She's a Cardinalli and doesn't walk out of what that means!"

I pushed him away easily and watched him slump, red faced, into his chair. "What does it mean?" I asked. "Did she know it meant her life was all worked out for her at meetings? Right down to the voting about paying her ransom. How about that?"

His expression told me all about how that hit, and he didn't like me at all. He picked up a pencil, discarded it and casually put his hand into the desk drawer on his right. It was all too casual for me.

When his shoulder moved to bring the hand back out I said, "Easy, Cardinalli. You should take a long look at my right hand now."

Maybe my voice told him; his face got a quiet, controlled look on it as he shifted his gaze to my .38 when I moved my hat.

"The hammer is all the way back," I said helpfully. "I've got a full load of flat nose wad cutters in it. All I need is one, Cardinalli."

He couldn't control the twitch in his mouth as the lips pulled back in a tight smile. He wet his lips with the tip of his tongue, remembering what he'd hired. He made like a stone.

"Careful, Judas," he said. "That won't get us anything, will it?"

"It will keep you from being stupid, Cardinalli." I wagged the .38 at him. "This has a very touchy hair trigger. It is pointed right where it's sure to put a cup sized hole in your chest if I touch the trigger at all." I kept smiling. "Now what would happen if you scared me by hauling that gun out of the drawer? Or even if you manage to hit me with a shot through the desk? Either one would get you dead, wouldn't it? And just because you think that being Mafia means your daughter lives by your code too."

He bit at his lip and stayed put.

"I'm not saying she didn't. I'm just an interested party looking at all the angles. All of them. I don't insult anybody or their codes when I look. I just question them all."

"Don't question Sandy's loyalty to me," he said stubbornly. "I can see your resentment after that Swan picture and having Luciano on you, but I swear no one is playing games, as you say."

"Don't swear to anything," I told him. "Just take your hand out of the drawer empty and slow. I'm pointing this at you just to stay alive."

He managed a laugh that broke and rasped away dryly. Then he put his hands on the desk, slowly.

"I wanted to scare you, that was all. Teach you that I wouldn't stand for insults or insinuations."

"That surprises me, Cardinalli. You can pass it on that it doesn't pay to scare me. I just get nervous about guns, and then someone gets dead because there is no way I can ever be sure that it's a scare, can I? I'm not even a little bulletproof."

Cardinalli wet his lips again, in control of himself now and watching me ease the hammer down on the .38 in my hand. "Fast," he said. "I never saw you reach for it."

"This isn't a fun way to make a buck, Cardinalli. Especially when no one seems to be passing on the truth to you. The .38 has been in my hand under my hat since I sat down to rub a few tender spots. I'm smart enough to know you'd do something to stop it. You're the type who can, and might, stop a man permanently for just a small thing. You can say the right word, and someone dies for it. I don't care for the idea of dying over a few questions you wouldn't like."

"It was a scare I had in mind."

"Scare then," I said. "I don't like to get scared like that either. You pushed me into a job I don't like and didn't ask for. I don't even know who'll get shot next in this mess. So don't try any more scares, or pressures, or any games. I get this way on a contract. I won't drop it unless you say so and pay off."

"I need you," Cardinalli said. "I can forget this happened today. I'll try to answer any question you still have."

"That's big of you," I said and glanced at the other picture from my jacket. Then I shrugged and put it back into my pocket. Cardinalli wasn't ready for that one yet.

"I think we covered enough questions for now. I'll be back again if I have something, but I still say pay Luciano off. That's your best choice, looking at the time we have left. Don't second best the kid with me."

He ignored it. "I can stall him some," he said. "Not long, but some. If you and Kincaid team up, maybe . . ."

"Go ahead," I said, "stall. That don't make me like Kincaid enough to cover my back." I shook my head at him. "If it works out that way, I'll keep him where I can watch him."

He still hadn't moved his hands on the desk as I went out. It had been sticky business but not as bad as the second picture could have made it. Cardinalli had lived his code so long that he believed it, and the second picture would have made him kill. It could still make him do that.

It could make him do a lot of things. He was a Mafia expert and knew how to get what he wanted. The show in his office could have been an act. There was nothing I would bet on just then, least of all Cardinalli's concern for his daughter's good name. He wasn't worried enough about her life to suit me.

CHAPTER SEVEN

At times I feel like a boy who has just discovered he has a deep rooted, suicidal urge and can't wait to try it out. I had enough people mad at me here to satisfy any form of self-destruction complex. It seemed like a good idea to catch the next plane out of the city, instead of driving toward Highland Park with little hope of making any new friends.

Since Bello and Potts, I shared the feeling with the grapevine that my life expectancy wasn't likely to be any long, dull stretch of time. I would have liked to pass the word that I was willing to live and let live with the second string boys. All I wanted was to get the girl and to have Luciano do his own dirty work. It was a thin wish, since I was in fact playing on Cardinalli's own second string. I could see little hope of getting the two racket heads together, where all of us second stringers could watch some blood leak from the top for a change.

These thoughts kept me from remembering that I

was on my way to contrive more lies if need be, to engage in any crude form of pressure that might be needed and generally to do anything necessary to further my own job—namely earning five thousand more iron men.

I relaxed with the drive and sensed the change in the city between midtown and Highland Park. It's abrupt, like slamming the door on a dirty spot behind you and finding yourself in the subdued, sultry living that only money can buy. Here people could afford big lawns and air conditioning. I was there only by the grace of Cardinalli's problem.

I tucked these thoughts away when I turned into the driveway of Cardinalli's home. Fighting down one last urge to leave for Mexico or some such place, I watched the house for a moment, then eased out of the car. I did not like to think I might find a lie in Cardinalli's last talk, but I went ahead and looked for one anyway.

The place was a Georgian, two story house with a large lawn around the half-circle driveway. My Ford looked out of place in the drive. I knocked, then spotted a door bell and rang. There was a damp, sweet smell of cut grass that was easy to enjoy. A maid opened the door, and I asked for Katie Dagerra. She let me inside to wait, while she vanished toward the rear of the house.

There was a double staircase to the floor above and fine carpets everywhere. What I guessed to be the den and library was finished in something like Spanish oak and an appropriate collection of antiques. I couldn't guess at the price of everything I saw, but I assumed Joseph must have a taste for expensive things.

When Katie Dagerra appeared, I figured she was one of the more expensive items the place had been supplied with. What she figured me for, as we studied each other, is anyone's guess. She had the brightest, steadiest, dark eyes I've ever seen. They had a deep glitter that belonged behind a gun at the kill. Other than that, she was strikingly female: poised, good looking, with a body that made your hands want to grab.

I wanted to grab, but I'll admit that her eyes could cool you off if she wanted it like that. She gave me a look that put me in the hired boot-lickers group which made it a little hard for me to remember that she was on the payroll too.

"What can I do for you, Mr.—"

"Jones."

"Mr. Jones then," she said, acting like she'd found me under a rock. She probably could read men pretty well, if she'd been around Cardinalli very long. I knew I had to be pretty good to bluff this one. Cardinalli hadn't exactly given me the go ahead for this chat. She asked me again what she could do for me.

I said the only thing I could. "You can tell me a few things about Sandy. You were her, uh, companion around here, weren't you?" I expected some sort of reaction from her but drew a cold-eyed blank. Not a quiver jarred her poise. I gave Cardinalli credit for picking a cool one to mistress his home.

"I don't believe we have anything to talk over about Sandy," she said finally. "I'd suggest you talk to her father about her. Who are you, anyway?"

"I'm Jones, remember? And let me tell you something, Katie girl. I work for Cardinalli just like you do. So give me credit for having talked to him first. Now I want to talk to you."

She stayed cool and thought it out. Her response to my questions was all right, but it was not really worth a damn when she had to guess what Cardinalli might want and she wasn't sure how to handle me. Maybe I was supposed to get the red carpet or maybe the bum's rush, but no one had told her which of the two to offer.

"The phone's right over there," I said. "Cardinalli was in his office not more than a half hour ago, so if you can't make up your mind, call him. I don't have a lot of time to spare, and Sandy doesn't have that either."

She considered that for a while as she studied me. I had the feeling that she knew the price of my suit and the caliber of my gun before she said, "This is about Sandy then? I think there's very little I can tell you, but you haven't told me what you are yet."

"I'm a guy who's getting a complex about being given a runaround when I'm supposed to be spending my time finding Sandy. Would you want to help me with that, or do I call Cardinalli, and we let him tell you to be helpful?"

"You won't make that call," she said evenly. "I think that if Joseph approved of this visit, you would have had him call before you came over. I don't think I should talk to you."

"Can you afford not to, Katie?" I asked. "She's been snatched, and he wants her back. Would I know that if I didn't have the job of getting her back?"

She shrugged.

"It's up to you," I said. "Do we talk, or are you just the silent, bedside decoration around here?"

Her face was quiet behind her cold voice. "I'll talk to you if I must. I'm not his puppet, as you evidently are."

"Right," I grinned. "He pulls the strings, and I do what I think I have to."

"That's an interesting approach you have, Jones. Does it work often?"

"Sometimes," I said. "Maybe this time it will."

"For the sake of argument, why do you think I'll tell you anything? I can still tell you to get out."

I nodded. "But you know I'd be back, don't you? And you would rather handle this without being told what to do."

"And what else?"

"Maybe I think Sandy is getting a short sellout and it shouldn't happen to a kid."

"A woman," she corrected. "Her age didn't have anything to do with it. She was a woman in every sense of the word."

"Should it mean something to me?"

"A reason to know that you're not looking for a little girl."

"That depends on how you look at it, doesn't it? This isn't a game. Luciano's not exactly what you'd want any daughter to be with."

"And you're supposed to get her back to save her that?"

Suddenly I was tired of the banter. I didn't give a damn about explaining myself anyway, and I was willing to rack this one up as a dead end too.

"I'll try to get her back—for money, Katie, cold, crisp cash. I couldn't care less if I save her from anything short of dying when I do it. I made a mistake thinking you might make the job easier." I turned toward the door.

"I told you I'd help if I can," she said. She nodded to a parlor type room off the hall. "We can talk in there."

It wasn't a long talk. I told her about the same thing as I'd given Cardinalli, only I left out the bodies and bombs. She listened well and didn't say anything until I finished.

"I'm afraid I haven't any idea who Sandy saw away from the house either. Billy Swan isn't a name I'd forget. Is he important?"

"Not now," I said. "But he was one of them who picked her up. An old friend turning up sort of thing." I waited a moment. "How were Sandy and Cardinalli getting along lately?"

"Why do you ask?"

"He's not paying the ransom, is he?"

"He can't! Besides, he hired you."

"That's damn little to do if I can't come close to her. He could have saved his money on me so far."

"But he's trying, isn't he? Who in hell are you to be a judge?"

"I'm the one who didn't want it and has to make it. I don't like flops at these stakes. She needs some breaks that he isn't giving her."

"Can't give to her," she corrected. "It wasn't all up to him, like he has a free hand there."

"He's as free as I am. All he's tied up with is a code."

"It worries you?"

"When it affects me. Maybe I don't like losing. At least I don't like losing five thousand bucks." I shook my head. "You haven't told me how they got along yet."

She was smart enough not to put herself in a bind. "That doesn't come under things a mistress should know, does it? I can't talk about their personal life."

"And you don't take any chances with this soft little deal here either. Is that it?"

"That's it exactly," she smiled. "But don't get raised eyebrows over it. I only sleep with him; you're the one who'll risk his life for him." She gave me another smile. "No, I won't forget how nice it is here. It's worth keeping."

"Okay, so we're both a whore of sorts," I said. "We sell a service, you for security and me for cash. I'll make a guess at what you won't tell me though and say that there wasn't any ideal father-daughter relationship around here. It doesn't give me anything I can use. Only a lead to her friends would help."

She shrugged, not committing herself, and asked, "Have you ever wanted something very badly, Jones? Well, when you do get it, you'll do anything to keep it."

I watched her and knew she was talking about Cardinalli and her own presence here in his house. I just shook my head. I didn't have any need like she had. My contract pay gave me all the security I wanted.

"That's what being here is to me," she went on. "From a strip act in one of his clubs to this, what I have here, is why I don't know *anything* about their personal lives. I only fit into one part of living here, and I'm not nosey."

"Does it make you spend a lot of time not liking yourself?" I asked.

"Do you ever really like yourself, Jones?" she wanted to know.

"Not much of the time," I grinned. "Damned little of it, in fact. Only remember that I pull my own strings. They don't have me in their hand like I was family. It's not a 'until death parts us' deal." I paused a moment. "They can't scare, impress or even surprise me most of the time, Katie. I've known the organization too long for that."

She smiled, and nodded.

For what the talk got me, I might as well have saved myself the trip out there. But Katie Dagerra was a better way of spending time than what I was used to. She didn't try to hide what she was to Cardinalli or the fact that she wouldn't do any talking that might upset him and send her back to the strip shows and the loneliness of the bright lights.

"Well, I'm satisfied with what I got," I said.

"And what's that?" she asked.

"Just a guess. You didn't say it; Cardinalli and Sandy not getting along just figures out like that. Now I can go find Kincaid and do some more guessing.

"You must want that money a great deal."

I picked up my hat and went out without answering. What do you say? Maybe offer an argument about the different price range of our contracts? Anyway, I'd sold too much of myself to know when the price was right. I was only certain that the price had never been right for Sandy.

I drove back into the city and found the rain had come back with me, filling bars and emptying sidewalks. It was great weather to think in. All I needed was a way to think all my loose ends together. It made me uneasy to have a contract and nothing to go on. Well, almost nothing, because I still had the photo I hadn't shown Cardinalli, and I had whatever Lieutenant Thierney decided to hand over. The catch there was that I needed to stay clear of Thierney too, now that he had Bello down in the morgue.

I had a small edge where Luciano was concerned. He was still laboring with the thought that I knew something worth killing me over. It was an edge unless I gave into the idea that Luciano simply wanted me good and dead and couldn't have cared less what I knew.

But what in hell was it that I should know? What meant as much or more to Cardinalli as his daughter's life? Thierney might have given me an answer with his news that Luciano was a very lucky hood with his takeover grabs. That sort of luck in the rackets called for inside information. I could fit that jacket onto Cardinalli just fine. He would want the informer in his bunch as much as he wanted his daughter back. When you got right down to the tacky part of it, I'd bet on his putting Sandy as second choice to what was eating at his power from the inside. There had to be a loose answer somewhere that I hadn't found yet.

I decided to do some more looking. I parked the Ford to call Butcher, who helped none at all and gave me the happy news that Thierney wanted to talk. He also gave me the address of a bar where I'd better meet the good officer, or there would be some loud whistles blown on me. I made it over to the place in ten minutes. I found Thierney as I pushed through the doors.

His eyes watched me come in, but his expression didn't change. He just nodded when I sat down across from him and said, "It's nice you could make it. I thought I might have to invite you to a talk the hard way, with a pick-up warrant."

"Any reason why?" I wanted to know. "Or is this just one of your off days?"

His eyes matched the tone of his voice. They carried a flicker of cold light that fit a hard cop. I was not exactly a virgin when it came to inquiring cops.

"I got a body for a reason, punk. I got one in the morgue, and it's a toss-up if another will be going there. I am up to my ass in good reasons to pick you up. It's peculiar how these two had their troubles come up while they were looking for you, isn't it? How did you do it?"

"I think you lost me, cop. Let's try it over and tell me who in hell we're talking about this time."

"Why Mr. Potts and Mr. Bello, of course. Your old back alley counterparts. I even have a fair description of the man who did the job on them. You'll love that and the fact that it was a nasty, cold, little knife job." He chewed at his lip and made me wait. "You fit the description real good. Want to tell me if you knew these two?"

I grinned at him. "It's all news to me, Thierney."

"I thought it would be."

"So what do you want? They were looking for me and had an accident. I don't think I'll cry over it."

"Quite a few of your friends have accidents, don't they?"

"I don't have any friends."

"You shouldn't," Thierney said. "The truth is I can't pick you up on the knifing unless I stretch things some. That's why I wanted you here. I think you didn't pay attention to our talk the other day."

"Didn't I?"

"For some reason you didn't get the part when I told you not to let me find any bodies near you." His eyes thinned down to lines. "Potts and Bello are unpopular here in the city, but if I stretch and push some, they are enough to pick you up. I'm letting that ride for now, but don't let it become a habit, Judas."

"Listen, Thierney . . ."

"Shut up," he barked. "I'm not quite done yet! If I could get Potts to finger you I'd have you in the slammer now! You remember that!"

"How could I forget it with you around?"

"You seem to manage things like that all right," he said. "Now, what's this information Butcher wants on Luciano's property?"

"Ask Butcher."

"I'm asking you. I want to know if it ties in with the murdered girl at the hotel."

I thought about it. "Not directly," I said, wondering if he could spot the lie.

Thierney let it pass. "Luciano has some property, you know. A hunting lodge up north."

I didn't answer him, and I hoped the nod I gave him covered the tightness creeping over me. He did a close face study on me and scowled, started to add something and stopped. Then he said, "Butcher asked for that favor, Judas. Don't be using him so much, and don't push him."

"He's a big boy now, Thierney. He don't push easy."

"Yeah, and you're a bastard on people," he said and slapped his hat on. He looked thoughtful. "I may get you yet, Judas. I'll wait."

He started away and came back saying, "Butcher's got that address on Luciano's property. When you get it, start remembering I'd get unhappy as hell if he left town with you. To start with, I'm unhappy that he even knows you."

I had myself a drink when he'd gone and stared out at the rain that seemed to never stop. It didn't matter if the pieces I had didn't fit now. They would never matter if the job could be finished with no worry of where it started. It was like reading the end of a book first.

As I left the bar, Luciano's lodge crowded my mind. I felt a slight lift in tension, knowing what my next stop could be.

CHAPTER EIGHT

I got myself far away from Thierney and his society honored code as soon as possible and drove across town to Butcher, to another code which grew on hate.

I wasn't surprised that Luciano owned a private bit of seclusion. He was the type who wanted a piece of everything for himself. It was part of the image, and there would be a certain satisfaction in sending visiting politicians and wanted hoods off to a comfy few days in the boondocks, all stocked and filled with the comforts of home, no doubt. Luciano was also the type who had to have the title for a place like that in his own name. It wasn't that he would go off the deep end and start yelling "look what I own." It was more like how nice it would be to see his name there and think "all mine" when he wanted to.

I was worried enough to sweat. My sort of worry does not come from being overly perceptive. It comes from the simple process of trying to stay alive and from knowing that you will not like learning a few of the facts before the job is over.

Facts are, at times, a pain in the ass too, because they will just be there, an unbent bit of truth that is not at all nice to have around. A fact like the single photo in my pocket made the pieces of my contract fit well enough, with some twisting of parts. They just happened to add up to the wrong answer—an answer that I wasn't looking for at all. When you have bothersome facts like these around, it boils down at times to how much you know about people. I couldn't shake a distinct feeling that Sandy wasn't really all that pushed for time now.

I parked the Ford near Butcher's place and got out to walk a few blocks while I shook down my lop-sided views. Habit made me check the place for a set-up while I did my own back checking for a tail. Finding nothing, I decided that Kincaid was either lousy at watching me or was content to guess where my search would take me. There was also the chance that he was sure I'd be around for him at the finish. Possibly he was at some hotel, with a bottle and a blonde, waiting for that call he was sure I'd make. Or maybe he just knew that it made me nervous as hell to have him running around loose and out of sight.

I waited through the noon hour and watched the eight to five boys clear out of Butcher's. I had the feeling that I was watching more than a bar. It was a hiding place for some old infamy that had been tired and used up until I came around to drag it out.

Between my thoughts and the rain, I didn't feel up to seeing Butcher in the bar, so I asked him out for a meal. It surprised me that he accepted with his face as scarred as it was, but I suppose a man like Butcher can adjust to anything. The looks and curious stares he got never affected him.

There was also good evidence as he worked at a steak in a Loop restaurant that nothing affected his appetite. He knew that he had the information I needed to keep searching, and he was in no hurry to spill it. Not that he intended to hold out for a cash payment or anything like that. He was simply being an ex-cop who was used to milking his information for as much return news as possible.

"You ran into a dead end on every lead you picked up then?" he asked. "My stomach isn't going to love you for feeding it an eight buck steak to get the last lead around."

"It's Cardinalli's money. That might help."

"Not while I'm eating," he said and twisted his scar into a look of horror. "Now we know part of what you want, don't we? But when you buy steak there is bad news around, or you need more yet. In this case it's both, I think."

"Sure," I grinned. "I want the location of the lodge Thierney handed over and information on the place."

"Then you should be more friendly with Thierney," he smiled back. "The man is dedicated to his work."

"He's dedicated to the job of locking my young ass in the slammer," I said. "Where do you think I spent a cheerful hour this morning? Talking to him and hearing a cell door slam every second word."

Butcher studied me. "Did you know that he loves his lousy work? Except for too many things like Potts and Bello. It bothers him."

"That's bullshit. He'd sit on my chest and drink coffee off my face if I were dead. It bothers him about like it would a grave digger."

"It's no bullshit, Judas. He knows you're a pro, so why should he play games with you? He's told you how it is and what mistakes you make are your own now. Do you think he's feeding us information because he figures getting *you* is important? He's got a few bigger fish to fry if he can, or I should say to burn if he can."

Butcher tasted the brandy he'd ordered and tapped

his fork on the plate. "Let's re-hash this before you go off looking for Luciano's hideaway, all right? We'll dig out the parts that stink to me, as a cop. And on this, Judas, you have a lot of parts that smell." He paused to chew a piece of steak. "There's a stinking item like the roll call for the dead so far. Only one of those could I put close to who did it. So who do I hang the bodies on if I'm a cop like Thierney? Take Billy Swan. What's the reason for him?"

I sighed, "The reason there is that Luciano is a sharp and safety minded boy. Billy was a big help in getting the girl all right. But when that was done old Luciano took a long hard look at his help. He knew damn well that Cardinalli or I would get to Billy sooner or later. He also knew Billy would talk, a weak spot that he plugged neatly by shutting Billy's mouth for good. Chalk up one for Luciano."

Butcher nodded. "I didn't think it was Kincaid's kill for one reason; Billy knew whoever he let into that room with him. The lock wasn't forced, and they knew all about the decal on his suitcase. Kincaid was looking, all right, for both Billy and the girl. How about her?"

"Luciano again. Murders like peanuts—you get one and can't quit. He wanted her out of the picture to be safe. The ones who killed her were asking her what she had told me, not how much she knew about Billy's travels, like Cardinalli would want to know."

"Two for Luciano then," Butcher said. "He's a very busy man."

"You can give Cardinalli one too, I guess. The stoolie who put me onto Swan. I'd say Kincaid did that one for him. Old Nino was too likely to go back to Luciano and sell me if he could. Nino just didn't know someone was already selling me out."

"Like who?"

I shrugged. "Kincaid or Pappas maybe; they both have a fair reason to hate my guts. And then it could have been some back bar spook who added two and two and came up with a winner on Luciano's checkbook. All I know for sure is that it was fast as hell."

"That's three unsolved murders to upset Thierney," Butcher said. "I don't wonder he's touchy."

"Yeah," I said. "Dump Potts and Bello on top of that and he's got an even four homicides with a probable fifth."

Butcher forked another piece of steak into his mouth. Giving me a long look, he said, "But in those two cases at least we know what happened, don't we?"

"Do we?" I wanted to know.

"Have it your way," he said. "At least we won't worry about them now. But have you thought that taking those two out might make Luciano push for a fast answer on the girl? He lost his protection between him and you. It could make him eager."

"That's part of why I want to take a crack at the lodge now. I can't shake the feeling that there isn't any rush now, but I sure as hell can't risk being wrong. Luciano won't do a thing until Cardinalli gives him the final no. I think."

"So we're down to the short hair, are we? Luciano's lodge, and it's a jackpot or go bust play."

"I'll know more when I see it."

He grinned. "Not you. *We* is the word. I get in on the end of this, remember?'

I sighed and brushed at my hair with my hand. "All kidding aside, Butcher, if Thierney knows you're leaving the city now, I'll land in jail fast, and I damn well believe him. He said to keep you out of it, Red. No heavy work."

"But there was also another little promise. The one saying I was in on the finish, wasn't there?" He pointed his fork at me. "You don't call me tagging along while you collect your pay, do you?"

"I'd like to right now."

"But you won't," he said simply. "Your word has always been good, Judas. I don't think you'll break it now. Promising Thierney to keep me out and me promising that I'd be in at the finish is sure as hell going to bend it some, isn't it?"

"Tacky is the word," I smiled. "A hairy bitch, but for one word. I said you wouldn't be in on anything heavy. No kicking down doors and that sort of thing. No close up bang-bang at all, in fact."

"What does that leave, Judas?"

It was my turn to grin and study him. Butcher had picked up a lot of grim talents from life. It was one of his deadly ones that interested me.

"Butcher, do you remember telling me once what you did during the war?"

He leaned across the table and tapped my plate. "Judas, it's been a long time. Don't count on me a lot there."

I thought it out again and tried to tell myself I didn't need Red, but the thoughts kept blurring and shifting back to two patterns. There was a fifty percent chance I'd need Butcher there or I'd be dead. If it went the other way, I wouldn't need anything but my .38.

"Butcher," I said, "all I'm going to bet on you is my life. So if you're rusty, get some practice. If you need any cash for the gear, let's hear it."

I should have been feeling some of the sweating that goes with the end of a job, but all I was feeling was a gut coldness because Butcher needed to be there. It was a shaky contract, and it put the wildness in me just beyond the time I had to reach for my .38.

"Christ," Butcher said. "Do you really think we'll have to do it like that?"

I knew he was pushing me now, doing what he could to make himself sure, but I couldn't give him that much. All I could do was give him a hand in the end, and if the right faces were there I'd need him. If they weren't, we'd play it by ear or by .38 maybe. It all depended on who turned out to be the most surprised.

I said, "Count on it being like that. We've got to do

it my way. Now let's have the rundown on Luciano's lodge."

"I don't suppose that the town of Beloit rings any bells for you, huh?"

I waited.

"All right, it's a small resort town on the Wisconsin-Illinois border, covers some land in both states, in fact. But for all purposes it's a resort town, one not known for any attention drawing excitement other than the usual local stuff most towns got. Beloit is a pretty average town and in good fishing country to pull in some heavy tourist trade. That makes it easy for visitors there who don't want attention. This make sense to you now, Judas?"

"It sounds like isolation equipped with an ideal spot to get lost in," I admitted.

"Okay," he said. "Then we add to that picture an all season lodge up on Smokey Lake, twenty miles out of town. Only two small resorts on that lake, friend, and you got a nice piece of solitude."

Butcher grinned after his research was out. Then added, "It's a lot of ground for one man alone to cover."

"I'll be paying that visit with a friend," I told him. "We'll likely be able to keep things interesting for a while." I grinned at Butcher. "You wouldn't expect me to do it alone when there is such eager help as Kincaid around."

It took Butcher a long time to think it out and grin. "Sure," he said. "You should really let Kincaid work off his eagerness. Just like I'll be working off mine. Let's hear what's on your mind for me."

I gave it to him simple and didn't paint any fun time in at the other end. It was clear, cold and dirty. It took five minutes to tell. He knew he wasn't being offered any fun and games when he thought it out.

Then he said, "I'll be there, Judas," and he left it at that. He finished his meal and studied the location on the map he had with the reluctant compliments of Thierney. And then he just studied me a moment before he nodded and left.

I watched him go and hoped that there was good reason for my faith in his past skills. His own faith in them was slow in showing. But then too, I was eager. I had to be to put my life on the line if he slipped. I had that on the line in a few other places, too. I played a risk with Cardinalli, Luciano, Kincaid and maybe a big one with Thierney, so Butcher wasn't a bad choice at all—not when he had his hate to keep him going.

The total I was betting on was pure guesswork: one photo and a lot of guessing to use at a maybe finish. Sometimes you can add up a contract for weeks and not like the answers you get. I shrugged and said to hell with it, as I went out to find Kincaid.

For a man who was being paid to watch me, Kincaid hadn't been any ball of fire during the past days. In fact, I'd only seen him work at it once, which could be some sort of a record. It could be, until you consider the possibility that Pappas or Cardinalli could also have him working at other bothersome things, too. Then it wasn't a record—just a surprise that he'd found time to watch me at all. It depended on how you wanted to think about it. I thought about Kincaid being a very busy man and put in a call to Cardinalli, who was likely keeping him that busy.

With the address of the restaurant I picked, it still took Kincaid the better part of an hour before he sat down across from me and waited with a peeved look while I studied him.

"What is this?" he wanted to know. "I call the boss and get told you're waiting for me here. You trying to be funny? I knew where you were."

"Sure you did," I said. "You haven't been behind me since the first night, baby. It's either that or you couldn't follow a two year old across the street. That leaves one thing, doesn't it? You can be working it like your own contract and guessing at where I am."

He folded his hands in front of him and leaned his elbows on the table. "Maybe I was," he shrugged. "What of it? It should make you happy as hell not to have me around."

I smiled at him. "That's funny," I said. "It doesn't make me happy at all. Now why is that? It could be like you get paid for watching me, baby, and when you're doing it right, at least I know where in hell you're at. I don't like the idea of you turning up as a surprise where I don't expect you." I watched him for a long time and finally added, "I don't like that idea one bit."

"So you don't like it then," he said quickly. "Okay, you stop playing games. You spend more time at losing a tail than you do at going somewhere. I ain't got time to play at following you." He managed a tight smile with that. Then "What is this besides a bitch that I ain't in your back pocket all the time?"

"It's a new game," I said, watching him over my cup. "It started when you came in here and sat down. We have suddenly become tight friends, baby. The kind that are always together. The new rule is that you don't even go to the can without me until this is over."

He looked like he didn't believe me.

"Real close," I nodded. "That's how you stay."

"Are you nuts or something?"

"In my old age, I'm being careful," I said. "I may be late, but now I'm careful."

"Luciano knows you," he reminded me. "Being seen with you is like sending him a telegram that I work for Cardinalli too. To hell with that."

I grinned at him some more. "That's right," I said. "Luciano doesn't know who you work for, does he? You're a real lucky boy at not being seen with the wrong people. It has to be luck when it only takes

Luciano a few hours to learn all about me." I waited a moment. "I wonder why in hell that is sometimes."

"Go ahead," he said, "wonder."

"I do, punk," I went on. "I don't lose sleep over it, but I wonder about that luck so much that I want you close to me now. Maybe I can learn that cute trick of yours."

"You'll tip Luciano off that I'm working for Cardinalli. That's what in hell you'll do! You'll blow the whole deal!"

I let him sit there and worry about our new togetherness for a long time. Finally I said, "The whole deal in a basket is to get the girl back, mister. You're going right along with me when I do that. It's too late for Cardinalli to start worrying about you now."

He caught that quick. I could hear his breath hiss out between his teeth, while I watched him slowly tighten up as the killer in him crept out. His eyes thinned down to slits in his face when he asked, "You know where she's at, then?"

I nodded.

"You're sure she's there?"

"As sure as I can be," I said. "If she isn't there, it isn't going to matter. She ran out of time, Kincaid; she's there or she's dead."

A smile crept across his face like a cold worm. "You mean *you* ran out of time, don't you? Cardinalli has to give his answer any time now."

I shrugged. "It's the same thing, I guess. Only we're going to be there first. Just us, and I want you to keep real close while we do it. You got that?"

"Yeah," he said, "I got it."

He looked like he had the idea all right. He looked exactly like he wasn't going to let me get over six feet away from there on out, at least not until we had the girl. It wasn't exactly a cheerful prospect, and it kept the hair on my neck standing up. About all that anyone could say for the idea was that he'd be easy to keep track of now.

At the same time, I had to admit that it wasn't going to be any hard job for him to watch me either. It seemed to be a toss-up if I'd gained anything, as we went out and got into the Ford. I knew for sure he wasn't the kind that you want running around loose, when you are trying to finish something without knowing where it started. And maybe Kincaid had an answer for me.

I kept busy by sorting out answers as we worked our way out of the city. There was no help in the ones I had, they wouldn't fit together, and yet there was that irritating little possibility that I was still missing the easy answer. Like it was right there in the rest of the mess, and I couldn't pick it out.

Later, it really didn't matter if I had. After all, you don't expect to shake out your own noose when you carefully provide rope for other peoples' mistakes.

CHAPTER NINE

When we were past the outskirts of the city, the rain found us again, making the driving slow. The low clouds rumbled wetly, with a sound that seemed to have a sneer in it. I thought about Kincaid riding silently beside me. I didn't care for the trip or company at all.

It is not my idea of fun to go off into the boondocks on contract. Anything more than a city park is wilderness to me. Give me the bad air and the city crowds. I need to drift with the people and feel the pulse that makes a city tick because the city is my hunting ground. I know how to use it. I doubted my .38 and the great outdoors would mix well, anyway. I hunt better on concrete.

I squinted at the road ahead, while a couple of details crawled around my mind with no ready slots to slip into. I knew they couldn't fit with the piece of picture I had, not in the middle of it where I'd started. I knew I was a fill-in piece then, one piece of a problem that Cardinalli would do anything to solve, but he wouldn't let me in on that problem. He gave me Sandy to work at instead. I couldn't see how they tied together without knowing what the beginning was, like Kincaid maybe knew.

The rain sounded like a snare drum on the car, as the tempo of the storm picked up, slowing my driving speed to a crawl. Nothing good seemed to be coming my way.

I glanced at Kincaid, who was keeping his thin-eyed silence like a stone while we traveled. It was getting harder to accept his being there just to watch me. Cardinalli knew I wasn't stupid enough to break contract. A gun doesn't do that and keep working. Still Cardinalli kept Kincaid around. I would have bet it wasn't because of his charming personality. That left only Kincaid's talents.

The logic in the guess was a little too real. I wanted to drop it there because Kincaid's talents were few and dirty. In fact, the only talent he had going for him, that set him apart, was the proven fact that there was nothing he wouldn't do for his pay. That covered a lot of ground, but Kincaid was the sort who could be sent on a crowd killing in an orphanage. "End any contract, in any way" was his motto, if he had one. That's how he worked. It made him special because most of us will draw our own lines in this business. There just wasn't any limit for Kincaid, who had the psychological makeup of a horror show. And Pappas had been the one to bring him in this, I remembered.

When four hours of driving were behind us, the weather handed out a reprieve. The overcast broke and we had a brief view of sunset before dark. I forced some of the tenseness out of myself and kept my mind on covering the miles and the road. We were past the large farm country, and a heavy growth of evergreen crowding the road had replaced fields and cattle. You still couldn't exactly call it turnpike driving, for all the improvement the better weather had made. There were just enough of those five house kind of villages along the way to keep the thought of some speed out of your mind. The narrow, winding road didn't encourage it either.

As it turned out, the hours had crawled around to ten o'clock before our headlights flashed on a sign that told me I'd reached Beloit. It was the first time I knew I'd been right since I took the contract. The place really was to hell and gone out in the boondocks. If you were going to hide someone, this was the place to do it. I drove the Ford around briefly to see what Beloit had to offer and then parked on Main Street to think it over.

Beloit now was a postcard copy of where everybody is told to go at vacation time. I could tell that I didn't like it already. It had a lumber and a feed mill and tourists as the industry to justify its existence in the middle of nowhere. There were rows of matching houses on the side streets, all obviously built by the same carpenter for dullness. Main Street was tourist gaudy, overfull of bars and arcades glittering newness that had been the sucker call for tourists since man first packed a bag and decided to travel off to far places.

You find that it's easy to tire of a nothing glitter that has all the charm of a carnival midway in a rainstorm. Fortunately, I knew my opinion of the town would have no effect at all on the citizens who were doing life or the visitors on a two week vacation hitch. In all truth, it was a way of life which Kincaid and I couldn't understand or blend into. For us, it caused a quick instinct of how vulnerable the town really left us. The warning, out of place feeling can be unhealthy for men like us.

A more casual but wary approach to this stunted version of a city paid off nicely, with the knowledge that there was no real need to feel like we were driving naked around the streets. It was only our own exposed feelings that set us apart. Plus there was a deep, hidden respect for small town cops who need only curiosity to make them ask pointed questions. A lack of anything else to do helped their question asking habits to be one sure pain in the ass.

Like a good workman, I did another hour of deliberate driving before I had the shape of the town in mind. It seemed unlikely to me that any of Luciano's disciples would spend a long time at the location eagerly. Guard duty on Sandy must rank low as a pastime.

There was some comfort in knowing that Kincaid was not overjoyed or relaxed either. However, I did not want him to decide it was a one man job and place a slug in my back. I wanted Kincaid stirred up with tension and on edge as long as possible because I knew it would affect his judgment. He had a loose and dangerous look about him which worried me. I'd played the contract out very loosely, with only a piece of the whole picture. Maybe Kincaid was the bright sort who casually let the work get finished before he played the final cards.

The contract seemed like an empty house which made less sense as it aged. You could go on forever, opening empty closet doors and getting a larger maze to explore, until getting out became more important than what you were searching for. The big flaw on a contract was the unwritten fine print which said the only way out was at the contract's finish.

At the very best, a broken contract would get me out alive, and future contracts would have to be things like Miss Average American having Mr. Average American knocked off for his insurance policy. That was cold reality. My own rules tied me to the Mafia like Cardinalli's code made him live for it.

Those were some good reasons for Cardinalli to be very sure I couldn't break contract or do anything but see it through to whatever ending would come. Those reasons also gave Cardinalli no reason at all for paying the price of Kincaid too. As I said Kincaid had only one reason to be kept in the contract that would make any sense. Just one.

It made me consider every detail I'd heard about him while I stopped and asked for directions at a service station and found a motel to check into along the way I wanted to go. His mood was ideal for a traveling companion as far as I was concerned. I'd gotten maybe a dozen comments from him since Chicago and would have liked even less. It could be a sign that he was thinking, and his face gave me a fair idea what his mind was on.

The double room at the motel rubbed his impatience into more conversation after I ordered ice and a bottle and generally left him with the idea that waiting was now on the schedule. He took the glass of whisky and water I handed him and sat down on one of the beds. "Okay, what is this now? Did we drive all over hell and out here so we can hole up and get stoned?" he asked. "It's about time I got let in on the game, Judas. The girl, you dig? How do you have that worked out and how do we do it?"

I grinned at him. "Oh, we don't do it, Kincaid. I do it. All I want from you is a backup gun. If I screw it up when the crap comes down, the whole shooting match is yours." I paused a moment. "This must be the place where I say how about it? Will you play backup?"

Kincaid studied his whisky and finally took a long swallow. "I don't like walking behind your ass like you think I'll screw the play up," he said. "I'm as good as you are, Judas."

My coat was on the bed. My Colt Cobra sat snug on its harness over my shirt with the clam-shell holding the revolver's grip only a twelve inch pull away from either hand. Kincaid was making me itch to use it and I let my hand drift over to my belt while I kept watching his eyes.

"I told you once how good you were, Kincaid.

That's why I know how you like your kills: tied up, knocked out or with their backs to you. I haven't heard anyone come up with the rumor yet that you tried out a gun who was expecting you."

"Bello's having his back to you didn't bother you any either, I hear," he said. "That was a chilly job."

"Yeah, one that they dealt, baby," I said. "They held all the cards and set up the play. I didn't walk in there as any stranger."

He licked his lips. "I still call it cold," he said. "Don't ride me, Judas. Just stay off my back about how I work, when you don't come out smelling like a rose on your own hits."

"I don't come out smelling like a baby butcher either, do I?" I asked. "It's a big grown up world where I work, baby, and no one has ever put me on a contract for a punk kid who pushed schoolyard grass and had a big mouth. I know about that one too, sweetheart. A real heavy contract, there, I'll bet. Your pay must have been all of five hundred iron men to take the risk of pushing a high school weed head."

Kincaid glared at me and chewed his lip.

"How about it?" I asked. "Or maybe you didn't get to collect that heavy loot because the wax brain who hired you only wanted the kid slapped around some. You must have got carried away with your work, huh?" I paused to grin at how it was eating at him. "You do have a heavy reputation all right, sweetheart. They got you down as the guy who'll take the jobs that are so rank that no one else will touch them." I let it eat at him while I tasted my whisky and then I rubbed his sore spots some more. "So you go ahead and tell me how goddamn good you are, sweetheart. You never made a cold play out front in your life. I'm not about to risk the girl to give you a start. Stick to kid killing, Kincaid, it's safer."

He let the glass go and came up off the bed. "You

son-of-a-bitch," he choked. "I'll take anything you can! I'll take *you* if I have to!"

That's when I made myself really grin.

He was tight lipped and narrow-eyed. He had gone white, watching me and remembering what he'd said. I let him stand there until he shivered with more tension than an overstretched piano wire.

"Here and now," I said finally. "Go ahead and take me."

I knew my grin hadn't changed, it felt quick-frozen on my face. I wanted him to try me so bad I could feel my breath snag in my throat. A sticky sweetness left my mouth dry. Even the cold grip that clamped onto my guts felt the waiting draw out. Kincaid was the type that a man in my business knows he'll meet sooner or later. The one I wasn't sure I could take. I knew he shot fast and kept shooting until you were dead, and I'd heard rumors about his practice every day.

The sweating I was doing ran down my back in chilly paths because a guy called Short Louie had once watched Kincaid at show-off practice and told me I was late as hell in beating him. In fact, he told me bluntly to shoot that thin, mean, pansy bastard anyway I could but never in an even play. Louie told me that over good booze and old memories, and I believed him. It came back to me clearly while I watched Kincaid.

You could form a theory, speculate, and guess, but the work got heavy when you were down to betting your life. The toughest bet to follow is a play that you called yourself against reasoning and old advice. In all truth, in the motel room, I wished sincerely that I'd taken old Louie's advice and words of wisdom to heart and put eighty grains of .38 lead through Kincaid the first chance I'd had. In front, in back or right through the ass, location didn't matter if the effect was right. Kincaid was a pure evil bastard who could only be trouble if you wasted a chance to make him dead.

My voice sounded like twigs breaking when I said again, "Go ahead, sweetheart, take me."

The tension in the room felt charged, like a bomb during the last, long seconds before the blast. My nerves felt like a static jolt of juice was playing jump wire through them while the final current was fed in. The sweat on Kincaid's face was frozen, like beads that wouldn't drip, and he quivered like a bird dog on point.

When he finally came unglued, it was like watching a statue coming apart. First he pulled in a deep breath. Then his jaw seemed to break away from his face, as he uncrouched and stood up. He blinked at me a moment, letting his tongue out to crawl over his lips and wet them. "I'll pull that last remark," he said. "You pushed me into it, Judas. Let's drop it."

"Maybe I don't want to drop it," I said, feeling sick, while my guts uncoiled. "You called it, and I'm here, okay?" How does it go? Drop it and I get to watch you behind me from now on maybe? Or do we finish it now?"

He found a tight smile. "We don't do either," he said. "I don't want a piece of you, Judas." He grinned. "The risk is too big and the pay too lousy to try. It's your own rule, isn't it: never take out a gun unless the money is there? The money ain't here, friend, and there wouldn't be any winner, so let's go to work on the girl and hate each other later."

I got my breathing straightened out and tried my whisky as I eased into the armchair to hide the twitching my legs were doing. I had made a long shot bet and had come up a winner on Kincaid.

The game gets a bit more binding when a real honest-to-God son-of-a-bitch is in front of you and the only judge is the question of who gets dead. There was one other thing that could make Kincaid a little reluctant too. He had lots of time to listen to the barroom whispers on my past contracts. He had all the time he needed to count the contracts and figure out what they had in common. Kincaid knew for sure that when I worked, someone turned up dead. To Kincaid, that sort of fact makes it real easy to back away quietly and bury a big hate. I knew he wouldn't try me like that again. It was a sure bet that I should watch him closely when he got behind me from then on. Kincaid is the type who lives on a special sort of hate, the sort that keeps getting larger and only ends when there's a dying to finish it. I knew that when *he* picked the spot for it, we would finish our little game. Until then, he'd do things my way. I hoped that gave me enough time to use him.

I finished my drink and made another one. "Make up your mind then. Are you going to back me up?"

His face showed tightness and waiting again while he propped up on the bed and tasted his new drink. "Make it easier for me to do, Judas. Would you back something you didn't know a damn thing about? Tell me what you know and I'll be there; keep your mouth shut and I'm not going to walk into it blind. I want to know where I'm at, man, and what I'm against. Who in hell plays this game in the dark, huh?"

I did, but I wasn't telling him that. I wasn't going to let him know there was about a fifty-fifty chance of Sandy being there at all. It would be pushing my luck a little bit too far. The vague picture I had of the whole set-up shifted around in my mind for a while, and I said, "Okay, sweetheart. Here's how it works. The girl is being kept around here all right. I'd say she's been here since they grabbed her, with no more than three of Luciano's boys around to watch her. I'm going to take her away from them."

"Yeah," he said. "But how do you *know* she's around here?"

"Where else would Luciano keep her? Hell, look around. You can pull isolation out of the air. Besides that, Luciano left Chicago today. He might be planning on being with the girl when he gets Cardinalli's answer, huh?"

Kincaid shook his head. "That makes four of that bunch now," he said. "And Luciano's no push-over. How do you figure the local law is going to take this target shooting?"

I waved it off. "No problem. They'll call it some crazy tourist's target shooting if they even hear it." I grinned. "I don't think Luciano will be calling for any cops, either."

He worked at his drink for a moment. Then he shook his head. "It's still a chance of going against four men, and Luciano owns some bad boys to fool with. It won't be any walk in and back out business."

"Did you plan on it being easy?" I asked. This is going to be a surprise party and that surprise party pulls a lot of weight. Why shouldn't it? They figure it's all been played real cute, and they haven't left anything but dead-ends back in Chicago. They're real proud of themselves, I think. So, it's going to be a jolt in the wilderness to get sudden company. I'll worry about Luciano, you just keep his boys off my back."

Kincaid got thoughtful for a moment. "How about a call to Cardinalli? We can have some of his people here tomorrow."

"His people are being watched and counted like steaks at an over crowded cook-out. That's why he hired us, remember?"

"Where's the girl at now?" he wanted to know. "The odds aren't so hot, even by surprising them. And what's the layout of the place?"

"You don't get the part of where she's at until we get there, and these odds are better than what we'd get in the city. I'll get the layout of the place tonight, and we get it done tomorrow."

"Just like that," he said and sighed. "I got a feeling it ain't going to work out that easy."

"There's a bus back to the city at midnight," I told him and looked at my watch. "You can be on it."

He held up a long-fingered hand. "Oh, I'll stick it out," he said tightly. "I just don't like the odds."

"They could get worse," I reminded him.

"Or better maybe," he said. "Shouldn't both of us have a look at this place?"

"Not a chance," I grinned. "If I blow it, you still can play, and it's all yours. If it comes off okay tonight, I can tell you all you'll need to know. We don't want any early shooting with the girl there."

He shrugged, too casually I thought, and paid attention to his drink. "I guess not," he said and smiled. "I don't like the odds, but maybe you can even them up some. I'm not sold on being a hero, Judas, so I like staying out of it just fine. But on Luciano you take a tip: get him first and be sure of it because he's the one who'll get the kid killed."

"Thanks," I said drily. "I hadn't intended to ask him out to a turkey shoot when I saw him."

Kincaid studied his watch. "Want me to give Cardinalli this while you check it out?"

"No calls, baby," I said. "If it works, we can hand out a surprise all the way around." I stopped talking until he looked at me. "You get that real clear. We do it now, we do it alone, and we do it careful for the kid's sake."

He jerked his head in a short nod and stayed silent. I worked my way through another drink and told him how long I'd be gone. I left him with the bottle and went out to the car with a hope that I could get a look at the lodge before we did have to do it.

I drove the Ford off a bit, parked it and walked back to wait under the trees near the motel. Kincaid's word was about as steady as a palsied dope addict in need of a fix. It took him twenty minutes to come out and make use of the pay phone next to the office. I didn't waste time wondering who he'd called. The only real truth he could pass on was that Luciano had started for the lodge today and the girl could be there. The rest of what I'd told him had been pulled out of the air to fill in the parts I didn't know because he needed a tight story. For all I knew, Luciano could have fifty men out at the lodge.

It was a great possibility to consider, if I wanted to think about kicking open any doors tomorrow.

CHAPTER TEN

Like a scattered puzzle, you find pieces of the answer in odd places. One piece of the puzzle which made Butcher's guesswork on Swan's traveling habits seem a little more solid I found clipped to an old candy rack in the display window of an all-night service station north of town.

The display was vacation decals. One with a simple design of trees and water and the words SMOKEY LAKE would have fit the scraped patch on Swan's suitcase for size. It was a small bit of fact to grab onto in the shifting, nightmare job I had.

The pump jockey looked disappointed that an oil change was all I needed, so I laid an extra five on top of the bill. "How far is it to Smokey Lake?"

Pocketing the money, he wiped the windshield while he talked. "Twenty miles or so," he said. "It's a sort of private lake with two resorts and a lodge. Guess they only take reservations out there." He studied the Ford's streaked windshield a moment. "We don't get much trade from there, but the lodge is a pretty steady customer. Those guys are in twice a week for gas and a night at some drinking at Pine Point. With the money they spend there, those two, I could stop pumping gas for a week."

His name was Charles, and he had lots of troubles that he told me in his insistent whine. His main problem was tourists who spent more money on booze and fun than they did on gas. I listened with interest to his gripes and learned that his watchful eye added up to two at the lodge. I figured it as two guards and one car, with them taking turns at a night off for booze at Pine Point.

He finished smearing the windshield up and said, "One of them's in tonight, too. Seen the car when I came to open up."

"Where's Pine Point?" I asked.

"Just up the road. These guys ain't friends of yours, are they?"

I shook my head, "Just wondering about the bar. Must be a good one to get all that trade."

"It's not so hot," he said. "If it were me, I'd stay out at that big fancy lodge or go to town."

Maybe I would too, I thought. Unless my job at the lodge was keeping watch on a seventeen year old, and my boozing was not on the approved schedule. Two men and boredom could make the risk of trips to the bar seem unimportant, but there were no small mistakes in the game.

I hoped that whoever was absent from duty at the lodge was enjoying himself. I didn't think he would be when I joined him. The station attendant was just getting warmed up on his problems when he paused for a second wind, and I drove off to find Pine Point.

The place was a lakeside bar with a swimming beach and trinket shop, plus the log and fireplace decor with stuffed fish and game heads to give the city sports the roughing it effect while they boozed in comfort. There were advertisements for every sort of outdoor agony, from swimming lessons to three week boat trips, scattered on the walls where they could be considered from the overstuffed chairs. The waiters seemed to be college football players in lumberjack get-ups. The whole scene had a garishly new flavor, like the pine log walls had been imported from a Hollywood movie set. It was a bit too woodsy.

I spent ten minutes sorting out the crowd to find the one I wanted. It was about as hard as picking a bookie out of the people at a church social. I got the bartender over and asked, "Anyone in from Smokey Lake? I was supposed to meet a friend from the lodge."

He nodded toward the one I'd picked and said, "Just Eddie there is in. I haven't seen Carl."

I grinned. "Ed's the one," I said, and watched him go off to draw more beer. At least I knew which of the two I had.

He wore the uniform like neon: dark suit, stingy brim and sunglasses, which made two of us in the room in suits and ties and very much out of place with the casual vacation set. He was trying his best line, and she seemed as interested in him as a bug collector with a new find. As I angled over, I wondered what Ed was saying his line of work was.

His eyes were flat as lead when he looked up to see one of his own kind there.

"Eddie?"

"Yeah."

"We just got in at the lodge. Carl sent me."

"Yeah, who's we?"

"The boss, Potts and Bello," I said, taking the chance. "He's wondering where in hell you are, the boss is."

I didn't give him any more and watched as he added it up. The names were good, but coming from a new face he got wary.

"What's Carl want?"

"That's not why I'm here. Luciano's why I'm here, okay?"

He glanced at the girl quickly and sent her off into the crowd, then said, "Boss didn't say he'd be up this soon." He looked like a dimwitted collector trying to figure out a shortage in the bookie take. He wasn't sure of anything. He was just getting a small, warning feeling that something wasn't right. Luciano's name was enough to make him ignore that when I said, "The boss don't like her left out there with just Carl, Eddie. We better get to hell on out there."

He glanced in the direction the girl had gone. His mind worked on that a moment like he couldn't handle two problems at once.

"Where'd you get it at?" he asked. "I don't place you."

"You won't," I grinned and winked. "Boss hired me out of St. Joe for this mess. We all can't get special jobs like you."

He liked knowing he was special and puffed up like a pigeon.

"Let's get this talk at the lodge over with, Eddie. And you and I come back then for some fun, huh? You can fix me up, can't you?"

"Ah, sure," he said. "These local pieces are easy. Makes me think I should pick a stable and start pimping sometimes."

"Yeah," I said. "You'd make a dandy pimp. Let's move it, huh?"

He fell into step when I started away and stayed quiet while we went out into the dark parking lot. He walked like he owned the sidewalk even where there wasn't any. There was an alien look to his strut, his clothes and even the slicked down hair on the back of his head.

I had a few inches on him, but his build gave him some thirty pounds past my weight. I wished I had a good blackjack then. I couldn't risk giving Eddie a chance to try me like Kincaid. He was old enough to know how it was done dirty.

I talked him over to the Ford and got in front of him to open the door like he had it coming. When he bent to get in, I was side braced and ready. I brought a sneak punch around. It was vicious and dirty and loaded with the ugly violence he could understand best.

There is some shock effect when an old pro is suddenly reminded that he's made a mistake. Helplessness is an ugly state when there is no way of knowing what comes next. The range of possibilities was big. Eddie could see himself as the main attraction in anything from a body cast to cement footwear, as he gagged from my punch and bent over like an open shotgun. I gave his guts another slam with my knee and clubbed him behind the ear to finish it.

As he wilted forward and down, I helped myself to his pistol and heaved him into the car by his belt. My work had taken perhaps half a minute. When I slid behind the wheel, the only sounds in the parking lot were the band's version of country music inside and the hooting of an owl off in the dark timber.

Eddie was rag doll limp in the car, spread out half on the seat and floor. When they're awake, you can make them sit on their hands. In Eddie's condition, I used his shoelaces to snug his hands together under his legs and propped him up against the seat where he looked like a graying, slack-jawed drunk. I couldn't find any spare sympathy in me for a working gun who'd goofed when a telephone call could have given him the right word. It was the luck of the rackets. He had relaxed on an easy job, and something dark came around to tighten up his game. Also, I could remember Swan's girl too well to feel one bit friendly toward him.

I put the Ford back out on the blacktop and ate up the night along the empty road, while I looked for a turnoff to dump Eddie. Five miles later I found a weed grown side road and eased the car along the bumpy ruts. There was a deserted cluster of derelict logging camp buildings which fit what I had in mind for Eddie.

I parked and cut the lights and listened to the night sounds out in the shadows around me. There was an owl hooting in competition with a dog-like howling somewhere near. There was no sign of a light in any direction. You could call it the local scene or the friendly forest if you wanted, but I didn't like the place one bit, and that was with my .38 out and the car running. I had the idea that Eddie would share that feeling when he got a view of the place from his well tied position.

I got him out of the car and into the nearest building. There was a clammy feeling to the place. I tossed my flashlight beam over the rotting boards and the fur-like patches of damp fungus. The air smelled of age and rotting dampness. The place seemed ideal for making old Eddie feel insecure. I waited for him to come awake and took a short look around before I went back out to the car to get the new working tool that Butcher had gotten me and that Eddie's friends were so willing to use.

I set the flashlight up like a spotlight on Eddie and opened the junky's fix-up kit in the light where Eddie could get a good look at the syringe and small tubes and could get the idea that what was in them was not likely to make him relaxed and cheerful. I didn't think Eddie had any experience at being a grand inquisitor with what I had, but as Luciano's man, it was just possible that he did have an idea how it worked.

He began to make feeble sounds and shake his head to get awake. I propped him up to watch his face as his eyes focused and crawled over the scene. He didn't like what he saw at all, but he dug down deep for some guts to get him through it.

"A sneak punch," he mumbled, like it had been a dirty trick. "You bastard, you sneak punched me."

"No shit. Did I?"

You had to spend some years at it, the listening part.

I'd listened to a few men answer questions in the past when there was pressure on, remembering them made it easy to pick up the shakiness in his words. There was a good edge of fear in his talk.

I didn't expect it to be easy, not when he had an old pro shell to crack, like opening a sealed box, before his words would have the right tone. I didn't have any doubts that his shell would peel, because there is no such thing as a man who won't break if you have the time and tools. I hoped I had them, for Eddie looked like the sort that you could blackjack your arms tired on without getting a peep out of him. It wouldn't be loyalty to Luciano or hate for me that would keep him quiet. It would be that rule he lived by that told him a snitch and a running mouth could get him killed, and that was a less cheerful event than being well pounded on. To get someone like Eddie loaded with the urge to ingratiate himself to you, there had to be a breath of something that was worse than dying. It had to be a new, unexpected thing that he couldn't fight.

"Ed, baby, Luciano is nowhere close to here, and there is not a swinging dick who gives a damn about you in forty miles. You are all alone, friend."

He watched me closely as I took the knife from my jacket and let the blade snap out. Then he said, "The lodge . . ." and let it trail off.

"Yeah," I said. "Someone out there will be damn unhappy about you getting so clumsy and not showing up, but that won't help you at all, friend. You're just playing ball with the wrong team."

"We could make a deal, maybe?"

I grinned. "No deals. You don't have a thing to deal with anyway. All I got to do is cripple you, or make sure you vanish."

He didn't like it, but he believed the sort of work he'd do himself. "I get a ride, huh?"

I patted his face to let him know he was guessing right and pushed the knife point into the wood beside the syringe kit and tubes. It looked like a back alley abortion set. I picked up a tube of clear liquid and held it in front of his face.

"Looks like water, don't it?" I asked. "But this is what will give you more than a ride, baby. *You* are going to take the long way around before you stop. Some of your pals used this on a girl I knew, so I'm returning the favor."

The sweat was working in lines down his face. His eyes stayed on the bottle. "What is it?"

"Acid, Eddie," I smiled at him. "We should have you knowing what to expect. It blows your mind, friend. Too much will do things you can't imagine."

He looked like he didn't want to know what even a little bit of the stuff did. It figured that he didn't know what to expect.

I already knew what you could and couldn't expect from LSD. I'd tried it once to see how deep they could dig with it, if I ever got treated to a question and answer session on it. I knew that if you didn't panic, there were some basic levels deep in the subconscious that couldn't be turned on. The idea was to send Eddie on his trip scared.

"This is fine stuff, Eddie," I said. "It opens your mind up, really makes you *feel* things. A bug crawling on you will feel like he's dragging a hot coal over your nerves." I paused and picked up the knife. "I'll play with you some with this then, and after you tell me all I want to know, I may or may not give you the big jolt."

Eddied looked like he didn't like his future a bit.

"Not an overdose, Eddie," I grinned. "Just a big jolt to make you feel like this knife is something to run from."

I patted his leg, and he jerked away. "Then I'm going to let you run, Ed. Out there," I said, and pointed the flashlight out through the open door. The beam cut the dark like a white hot rod until it lost itself in the twisted trunks and shadows of trees. "Tough like you are," I went on. "You should manage to run for a long time out there. But there's nothing to run to, Ed, just the woods and whatever will be waiting for you when you stop running. You can't tell what the smell of blood will bring out of these woods, can you?"

"Jesus," he whispered and sounded like he meant it.

"Yeah, it's even better than hanging a guy over a hot bed of coals and letting his brains cook."

He swallowed and kept staring at the syringe like he'd just found a Black Mamba in bed with him. Eddie hadn't tried any LSD, I guessed, because it *could* do things like I'd told him on a bad trip; it could dredge up all sorts of horrors. On the other hand, if he kept control, all he'd come up with was an unusual mind bender.

"A deal, huh?" Eddie asked. "We can make one, can't we?"

"No deals," I said and paused a moment. "I ain't got a thing against you personally. Maybe if you want to tell me a few things I could just make sure you stay here a while after I leave." I grinned at him. "Hell, after this blunder you sure can't go back to Luciano, and nobody would know you talked."

"What sort of things do you want to know?"

"The layout of the lodge and all you know about this deal on Luciano and Cardinalli's kid."

Eddie wagged his head. "I never been a pigeon," he whispered. "Do I look like a rat?"

"No, most stoolies look smarter," I told him, and picked up the syringe and a vial of LSD.

Eddie watched with his jaws clamped shut while I loaded the syringe with enough juice to blow a horse. He stank of fear, but he was the kind who would dummy up on the slim hope that I was running a bluff or that it wouldn't work. He kept staring at the syringe in bug-eyed doubt. He couldn't make himself quite believe that a needle would make him do what a gun or a knife wouldn't, and his jaws stayed clamped shut while I found a vein and slid the needle in.

When I stepped back, he said, "It don't hurt none."

I gave him a nasty grin. "You got about a quarter of an hour, Ed. Enjoy it before the fun starts."

He wanted to doubt me, but his eyes said he believed it.

From there on out, I had to guess at what Eddie was going through. Considering that he was scared to begin growing in him when his gaze settled fixedly on the with, it wasn't hard to sense the frantic tenseness flashlight and he felt a sensation like his brain had dropped into a long dark tube and was falling away from his body. His eyes stuck out like shelled eggs as I watched. Eddie was on his way all right, and he didn't know where he was going. When he began hallucinating it could be anything from rainbow colors of lights to a slimy blackness he'd find himself seeing and caught in, or seeing hair as new grass or wiggling snakes. A trip could go pretty far out either way. You might find something you didn't want to leave or a mind blowing horror where you couldn't get back.

I didn't figure Eddie was going to take the happy route while I listened to the whimpers escaping from him. I switched off the light and dragged my hand over his face in the darkness, knowing that it could feel like a wet snake or a hot wire brush to him.

The screech that came out of him made the hair stand up on the back of my neck, and I snapped the light back on. His twisted face was something you couldn't match in normal expressions. His voice was a harsh babble, spilling helpful news to ease some of the fear I'd planted. Eddie, it seemed, was a sidewalk loving native of well lit streets. In short, the dark scared hell out of him.

I started again. "How about it, Eddie? Want to tell me about the lodge and the Luciano and girl deal?" I had to say it slow and keep repeating it to make sure the question stayed in his mind. He didn't answer the questions at first because some ingrained part of his makeup kept holding out.

I gave him a few more tastes of darkness after that, while I grabbed and touched him out of the blackness until he spilled shrieks into the cabin that were gut tightening to hear. It would have been easier for Eddie to take if I'd made him talk with the knife.

But he talked, and when I turned the light back on, I'd learned most of what I wanted, but I didn't enjoy collecting information from a numb and panicked mind. I untied his hands and left him trying to hide in a corner with his feet still tied. I went back out to the car. It would be a long time before he came around enough to untie himself and walk out.

There was a bitter taste in my mouth. I kept hearing Eddie screaming at his fear in the dark behind me, while the car lights cut the black tunnel of the road toward the lodge and the night started to run out on me.

CHAPTER ELEVEN

Smokey Lake seemed to be five miles on the other side of nowhere. For the most part, the lake was edged with evergreens and covered with mist.

I guess you could call the mist a smokey look if you wanted to. Along with the night I'd had so far, all it gave me was a creepy feeling. Maybe it looked better in daylight, but there's not a hell of a lot you can do to add cheer to brooding trees and deep black water.

After a while, I remembered that I didn't have to get turned on by the son of a bitch anyway, and I put the car in gear and drove slowly down the beach road toward the lodge. Eddie's directions had been correct so far. I parked the car off the road to do the last quarter mile on foot.

It figured that Eddie's partner was one mad bastard by now and likely waiting impatiently for Eddie to return with the car. Since anger tends to keep a person alert, I didn't kid myself into thinking that there would be a content and dozing man at the lodge. There was also the chance that Luciano would be there.

I stayed at the edge of the trees as the road dipped into the clearing around the lodge. The building looked like a quarter of a million bucks worth of rocks and logs. It was a ski-type lodge with a hanging terrace. You could call it plain good building. It gave you the impression that it was comfortable inside. I hoped that Luciano was there and real contented with his private piece of nowhere. I wanted him slow and drowsy when his surprise came.

I listened to the night sounds around me and wondered where Butcher was. My eyes followed the tree line around the blind side of the building. Then I crossed the clearing in the thin moonlight and stood in the shadows of the lodge.

For all the effect the lodge had on you at first sight, it was still a gloomy place to be spooking around at night. It just wasn't the warm, cozy sort of place a lodge is talked up to be. I brushed the peeled log wall as I worked my way around to the lake side of the building, making mental notes on the location of doors and windows. I spent fifteen minutes at it and checked the connecting garage last. Looking at the moonlight patterns on the empty parking places, I had the odd feeling I was clinging to the underside of reality.

I made a half-hearted attempt to shake it and swore silently at the empty garage. No cars meant no Luciano. He'd either come and gone, or he'd never started for the lodge at all. Anyway, he wasn't there, and I could wonder if Sandy herself was. There hadn't been any sign of a light since I'd first seen the building.

I eased back around the garage and viewed the sliding doors under the terrace overhang with a reluctant interest. The glass looked like wide, black eyes into the building. I hadn't planned on any more than a look, and I felt uneasy about any change in plans that I couldn't pass on to Butcher. But the quietness of the deeper gloom inside the lodge was a good reason for checking it. Also, I knew that there was likely only one guard with Sandy, if she was still there. The odds couldn't be better for going in. I had to look now.

I could hear the growing sound of wind in the tops of the trees as I stole over to the glass doors and went to work. I was sweating before I managed to lean my weight in the right place on the glass and finally felt the door snap out of its slide.

The sounds seemed loud in the dark as I forced the opening and pushed my way into the lodge, feeling as though I had broken into a tomb. The place had a normal, lived-in odor, but the feeling stayed with me. My nerves felt like stretched piano wire.

I took my shoes off and slid my .38 out for the prowl. The dark of the lodge made me nervous because it would be tricky to shoot if I had to, and I couldn't hurry the chance of running into a bullet by getting clumsy. I padded carefully through the gloom and vague shapes of furniture in the living room. Feeling the live coal heat under the dead ashes in the fireplace as I passed made me feel creeping, cold toads start along my back again.

I grinned in the dark at the chance of finding someone in the lodge to have a long talk with, but the chance of getting myself shot also improved. It made me move a little more carefully. I am not eager for this sort of night hunting, not when a surprise can be the blast of a gun pointed at you from a few feet away.

I was clammy with sweat before I'd finished prowling through the lower floor. It seemed like I'd been in the lodge longer than the hour my watch indicated. I remembered the brief grayness of false dawn on the windows and knew that daylight would change the game. Then I'd be the hunted.

I made a slow, silent trip to the second floor stairs and started up. I felt as wrung out as a limp sock. I was running on frayed nerves alone.

The smells around me changed on the stairway. At the top of the stairs was the musty, warm odor of sleep mixed with smells of overused bedding and a vague perfume that put sharp jabs into my tiredness. Fatigue wasn't a luxury I could afford; it could lead to dying.

The night gives you a flair for hunting, an immediate sense of safety and danger. There was something alive and dangerous in the darkness of the second floor, and it built up an expectancy in me like a raw ache.

I waited in the silence of the carpeted hallway, like a cat listening for a rat in a garbage can. I made myself keep waiting because the time wasn't long enough for any second chances.

It was guesswork I had to take the chance on. Even with a lot of loose ends, there might be a possible pattern. That part of the pattern had sent Eddie on his trip to the bar, and I had provided a number of reasons for his not returning. It figured there should be only one guard left at the lodge. My .38 was slippery with sweat. I hoped like hell I was right. Remembering a single whisky glass by the fireplace helped me think so. A dull routine and good booze could make a man relax past the safety point, like Eddie had. Maybe his partner had decided that isolation and a locked room on the second floor were enough to keep a seventeen year old there. It was a solid enough pattern to make me want to believe it.

I wiped the sweat from my hands and wondered what Kincaid might be doing after a night of waiting for me. It would be nice to be sure that he was worried.

At present my thinking called for me to cat-foot it down the hall and wish Luciano's guard a cheerful good morning with a slug and to keep shooting as long as he twitched.

I waited and wondered where he was, because I wasn't wild about putting my dulled reflexes up against Luciano's baby sitter when he was fully awake and alert. He was likely dangerous as hell every minute then. I couldn't see any value in a cozy chat, especially when my urge for survival told me to find him slow and sleepy and to start shooting then. It also told me never to underestimate a bastard who made his buck like I did.

The rules were that I could call it like I wanted. I wasn't about to take in any more risks when I knew my tiredness was eating large holes in my reflexes and I'd soon be about as alert as a dead cat. I also knew that Luciano wouldn't have the man at the lodge unless he had proven his ability at assorted mayhem. He might be very good at it too. Best of all was knowing he wouldn't blink twice at a chance to kill me. That wisdom could make you pull a trigger fast, unless you liked the idea of dying.

The .38 felt suddenly snug and natural in my hand, as I heard the sounds of a bed creaking and feet on the floor ooze into the hall from a room on the right side. The faint sounds seemed loud to me. I guessed quickly that the open door leading to the bathroom at the end of the hall would be the guard's next stop.

I stayed just past the head of the stairs. The sounds of his waking up pounded in my ears. I felt only a bone deep desire to be done with it. The perfume odor belonged to Sandy in another room, I decided. I shifted my gaze back to the first door in time to watch it be pulled open.

My logic told me that the guard wouldn't carry his gun to the toilet. It also offered up the wisdom that an unarmed man would offer me little trouble. When he turned toward the toilet, I stepped out of the deeper shadows behind him and said, "Make like a rock, bastard. Don't even blink."

Luciano's guard was not working on my sort of logic. His motion never stopped as he went into a fluid, rolling dive and came up next to the wall, his pistol ripping the hall apart with its flash and lead that smashed through the meat of my arm.

I didn't feel at all like I'd surprised anyone with their pants down. Instead, he managed to surprise hell out of me, until his second slug hit the wall and made me flinch with the splinters which it drove into my neck.

He got up on his knees and put one more hole into the wall between us before I rested the .38 on the door frame and slammed two flat nosed, eighty grain slugs into his chest which tossed him back against the wall like he was doing a speedy backward leap.

I watched him ooze down the wall with the orange size holes pumping red and waited until his fingers twitched loose from the pistol grip. Then I managed to get a cigarette going and walk over. There was nothing to see about the guard. I dropped his .32 into my pocket. I began to feel the throb of smashed tissue where the bullet had gone through.

He'd come close to doing the job, all right, but Luciano would be finding himself short of hired help pretty soon.

After a while, you get a little sick from knowing that there is always someone who gets paid to do the dying. If you don't know why your guts knot up yet, you just wonder about the dead ones and hope that a week or so in a whiskey bottle will make you forget enough to work again.

I left him to bleed on the expensive rug. "To hell with it!" I told myself, and I went to search his room.

CHAPTER TWELVE

My search of the dead guard's room turned up a total of one key. The only thing it fit was the door to the room. All I needed now was for Sandy to turn up in an unlocked room. That would be a real laugh, but I couldn't see anything funny when I pushed the door to her bedroom open and met her frightened gaze.

Standing in the doorway of her bedroom, I could feel tiredness settle over me. Suddenly I didn't need to fill in any more pieces of the puzzle or open any more doors to form a complete picture. The end results were what counted. Sandy was one of the better endings I'd seen!

Lying there, she looked like the-girl-back-home type—all big eyes, and a body that didn't belong to any seventeen year old. I found out later that her face and body were the tools of her trade.

Leaning against the wall near the door, I made myself smile with what meager brightness I had. Sandy wore a fixed expression with a lost look in her eyes.

She didn't look happy or really scared or anything you'd expect waking up to morning murder. She looked like she had been waiting. I felt cold when, as I read the fear in her eyes, I realized she had decided the waiting was over with me.

"It's okay, kid," I said lamely and then remembered that she was a Mafia kid and shouldn't shake too easily. "The shooting in the hall just got you a ride back home."

She looked at me briefly, then at the arm that was dropping a steady patter of scarlet onto the rug. Since I didn't think she was overly interested in my health, I figured she just didn't want to look at my face much. There was still that sense of fear in her, though her voice was steady.

"That was Carl, then?" she said. "He's the only one here now. Is he dead?"

"I hope so," I said, resting against the wall. "And Luciano is due out here anytime, so let's get some things done before he gets here. Then you can go back to the city and dear old dad."

"Did he hire you?"

"He gets my bill, Sandy, but there's more to this than what he told me. Tell me how they managed to kidnap you and why, as a starter?"

I repeated what I knew about Swan's part plus a few details and let her take it from there. She started rattling on like she was talking her way out of a bind, saying less than Cardinalli had. It was close to babbling at times. I learned nothing.

The flow of words were not the response I wanted. Her tone didn't sound right.

"Hold it, kid," I said.

She stopped talking quickly and her stare went to my arm, which was starting to hurt like hell. I sighed and shook my head to clear it, then said, "Sandy, you've covered at least six of the questions I had without telling me anything. Let's go back, and I'll feed them to you in pieces instead of trying it all at once."

"But shouldn't you fix your arm first?"

"I should," I agreed. "You find something to fix it, and we'll talk during that." She managed to make a project out of it and delayed talking until the bullet hole was padded and pampered to where I knew I'd only be stiff for a week or so and I'd decided the slug had only smashed meat.

As she finished, I asked, "Did you know anyone besides Swan in the bunch that grabbed you?"

She looked at me oddly. "I knew them all, Eddie, Carl, Billy. . . ." She stopped. "What happened to Eddie?"

"I happened to him," I said.

"I only wondered," she said. "They didn't treat me bad."

"How about Luciano? Did you know him before they brought you here?"

"I knew who he was," she said slowly. "I used to see him when I went out with Billy, but I didn't meet him."

"Cadinalli wouldn't have liked that, huh?"

She hadn't relaxed any since we'd begun but Cardinalli's name made her tighten up even more. Her voice was thin when she said, "No, he wouldn't like that."

I kept it up while I put my jacket back on. "How about Kincaid and Pappas. Do you know them?"

"Only Mr. Pappas."

We spent a long time at it for nothing. "Okay," I said, "they snatched you and brought you out here, right? Was Luciano here then?"

She nodded thoughtfully. "He said that they wouldn't hurt me and that I could go home when daddy did what they wanted. Then they put me in this room, and I've been here for ages, with Carl and Eddie out in the hall to watch me."

I almost told her that she would be there a lot longer

too, if she was waiting for Cardinalli to pay to get her out, but I let it go with a sour taste in my mouth. When you're looking for answers, you learn that most people give away their lying by some little action or other. But finding the giveaway isn't easy. I knew I was getting lied to without knowing where. Sandy asked me if she had helped when she finished talking.

I shrugged and said, "Yeah, I damn near know less now than I did when I started. You might say it's a little weird to wrap up a job without knowing the reasons behind it."

She didn't even blink before coming up with an answer to that, "What difference does it make, if you get paid to take me home?"

It sounded like Cardinalli's sort of logic. Dollars bought work done, with no questions asked. But she should also know jobs that came with a smell could be handled with a .38 questionnaire.

Murder happened to be a trade where the hired man could reasonably ask why a job needed doing. When the reasons he was given started to stink, it was a good idea to look for some first-hand knowledge.

I thought about Sandy's question and decided that it did make a difference to collect for a job without knowing why there had been some funerals. I said, "It makes a difference because the right answers might have saved some work and some funerals. I don't like to overwork for my pay. And get this clear right now, kid, you didn't hire me, and I don't jump when you call, like Cardinalli's people do. I don't care what sort of bed games you play behind dear old dad's back either, but you are answers and cold cash to me, and I intend to collect both of those before you get back home."

The fear left Sandy's face and a few hard lines turned up around her mouth to spoil the girl-next-door image. She was a seventeen year old packed with thirty years of unwatered facts, and she hadn't learned any of them from fools, not in the Mafia. Now she looked like she had never been a kid, saying, "What's the matter, you don't make an easy dollar when you can?" She cocked her head, "Just get me home. Answers like you want don't spend any place."

"It's my bag," I said. "I'm queer for looking behind me and finding out why I've done something."

Sandy sat on the edge of the bed. There was nothing girlish in the way she showed enough bare skin to make you think the promised land was reachable. It was nice to view, but bullet holes and short sleep don't exactly make you start panting heavy over jail-bait. I didn't much give a damn what I could get from her besides my contract fee.

"You do things the hard way," she said.

"It works out better like that. How about when Luciano was here, did he say anything at all about Cardinalli, or why he pulled the snatch? Did he want a way into the rackets?"

"You know how that is, not even my father would tell me anything about his business. Luciano wanted money, didn't he? What's so hard to figure out about that?"

I grinned at her. "Maybe just how bad he wanted it. An up and coming punk just doesn't go and snatch Cardinalli's kid."

Sandy seemed worried. She knew every action to fit the mood she wanted to present, but she hadn't found a way to stop the flat, appraising look in her eyes. I wondered briefly how much I could believe of her story.

I watched Sandy a moment, then said, "You get ready, and we'll wait downstairs." I grinned, "I may even remember to ask Luciano how *he* had this nice little circus figured out."

She spent ten minutes dressing without bothering to ask me to leave the room, so I didn't make any attempt not to watch her. I got her downstairs into the living room, where she found a bottle at the bar and picked a chair near the fireplace to enjoy it.

I picked a location at the side windows to watch the lake shore road and cover the three entrances into the room. I rubbed my eyes and leaned against the wall. I tried not to think about the armchair a few feet away. I kept going over my talk with Sandy in my mind because it kept me awake while I watched.

I knew Luciano would have some answers. There was no doubt I was eager for a chat with him.

I rubbed the back of my neck and kept trying to keep a creeping sense of fatigue from taking over when Sandy's voice cut in.

"You can talk, can't you, mister?" she asked. "I've been in that room like I've been in another world. Now I'm out and don't even know your name. I'm curious."

The low laugh she finished with made me realize that her sudden change to a cheerful mood was due to the whisky bottle. Even though I could use some talk to help stay awake, I didn't want any chatty conversation with a well oiled piece of fluff who'd handed me some wrong answers already.

I agreed silently that maybe she did need a large dose of booze after the last few days. So maybe she deserved it and was just plain lonesome, but I was too beat for a tea-time light talk or for getting tied up with any other house games she might have in mind.

I studied her face and said, "Look, kid, I don't give a damn about your curiosity. Matter of fact, I'll be pleased as hell to see the last of you and collect my pay. But there's a few things to do first. Right now, I'm waiting to do one called Luciano. When that's all tidy and tended to, we can get out of here." I nodded at the bottle she was holding. "You can get stoned, but stay out of my way. And to satisfy your inquisitiveness, the name is Jericho, all right?"

"And I'm sorry I asked, all right?" she said. "Are you going to shoot him when he gets here? Luciano, I mean? I'm going to stay sober and watch, if you are."

My hands were clenched like I was trying to crack a handful of air. The idea of just locking her back up in her room was tempting. It took me a minute or two to talk myself out of that and decide that the talking might keep me awake.

"What happens to Luciano is up to him," I said. "He can play it like he wants to when he gets here. If he's real careful about digging out his gun and things, he might even stay alive to talk to Cardinalli, too."

The thought made me check my .38 and reload the fired chambers, thinking while I did that Luciano wouldn't see anything nice about talking to Cardinalli or to me, for that matter.

"Oh," Sandy said and looked thoughtful for a moment. Then she asked, "We could leave right now, couldn't we? He wouldn't have any chance to stop us then, Jericho. I'd do anything you wanted, go anywhere. We'd be safe." The tone of her voice pulled me around to look at her. She'd adjusted herself in her chair to make her suggestion hard to turn down, but her face was pale.

I shook my head and smiled. "You got it wrong, girl. I want to see him, not avoid him or meet him on the road leaving here. I've got a little personal matter to see him about too, something like his trying to get me killed a few times. So we don't want to run off and miss him, do we?"

She was silent a moment, then smiled slightly and asked, "Do you want a drink?"

I started to wave it off but decided that one wouldn't make me feel worse, and it might help. "Straight rum on ice, if it's there."

I watched her find it behind the bar and fix half a glassful over ice. It was a raw burn on the first drink, but it built a fast glow in my stomach. I reminded myself to take it easy. The steady throb of pain in my arm was doing part of the job of keeping me awake now, and I couldn't afford to stop the pain. Not yet, I couldn't.

Sandy studied me for a long while and then asked, "Couldn't you sit down and watch, while we're talking?"

It was a good question because I sure as hell wanted to plant myself in a chair, but that was just a little too much comfort for my schedule. When she moved a chair over, I perched on the armrest, while she sat a few feet away and steadily made a larger dent in her bottle.

I was beginning to wonder about little Sandy. She put booze away like a party girl, but it only seemed to mellow her to a certain point. She seemed sure of herself and how much booze she could handle. Also, there was a deliberateness to her drinking.

She knew every way possible to twist around in the Sloppy Joe rig she had on and managed to prove it by showing all she had under the slacks and sweater. She watched me with the expression of a broke hooker and finally said, "Let *him* do it!"

I stared at her blankly.

"Let daddy send someone after him," she said. "I want to get out of here, and you can barely stand now."

"I'll last, Sandy," I said. "You just worry about how you hold together. Besides, there's no way out of here without a car. Luciano will be here before we could call one out of town. So just drop it."

I went back to watching from the window and listened to her walk up beside me until her hips and breasts were warm pressures against me.

"You wouldn't regret leaving now," she said. "I could make the money up to you."

I grinned out of the window and shook my head. "People buy me on contract, kid, but even if I didn't lose a cent on Luciano, I'd wait for him. Maybe you're good enough in bed to make up for the money. Okay.

But there isn't a bit of fluff working a mattress who could make up for his trying to kill me, so don't try conning me to leave early. Just snug your pants up and go sit down. You'll get out of here."

She gave me a dirty look and found a chair ten feet away to sit and pout in. I went back to my window view.

The throbbing of my arm counted the minutes with me. The road blurred out of vision when I stared too long. My thought on the past days of the contract crept back. I spent an hour on them before I saw the car coming.

It was just a few flashes of color through the trees across a bay of the lake, but my mind clicked, registering Luciano. I watched Sandy from the corner of my eye and saw her silently boozing.

I left my view at the window and walked thoughtfully over to Sandy. "I been thinking. Maybe you're right at that. Why should I take the risk on Luciano, when there's you, plus fun and games with no risk connected." I smiled at her. "Yeah, and I'm tired like you said, so let's get the hell out of here."

She switched on a smile which could buy her a lot of things. When she stood up, I hit her. It was a solid punch that knocked her cold with the smile still on her face. I moved her to where she couldn't be seen from the doorway. I took the chair she had been sitting in.

Her gun was down beside the seat cushion where it would be handy. A nine shot toy, or woman's gun, that could kill hell out of you at close range. I decided she had picked it up during the time she'd spent on my arm. I emptied the pistol and grinned as I went back to wait for Luciano. There wasn't going to be any surprise help for him now. I was one problem he was going to have all by himself.

Time began its usual act of seeming slow. I watched the road where it came into a clearing and guessed at the distance Luciano had to travel. He was a long minute overdue.

After the past few days and the tone the job had so far, I somehow kept expecting him to vanish. I eased my .38 out as I moved away from the window. It was almost too much to see something go right, but the sound of a car door being slammed outside the lodge put Luciano exactly where he should be.

I watched the doorway to the room silently. The tightness in me made my neck taut. A cold spot settled back into my guts. There's a sort of electric tension that creeps over your skin when you're close to the finish of a hunt. Luciano was close enough to make every nerve quiver when I caught myself thinking about what he'd likely do.

I was scanning the three doorways into the room. I felt a passing lick of weakness in my legs when the front door handle moved. I swung my .38 to cover that one and waited while it opened.

Luciano had made the first two steps into the room when he simply dug for his gun.

I didn't need to say it very loud. All I had to do was pull the .38's hammer back so he could hear its double click. It must have sounded like dying to him. I told him it was very close to that.

"Keep reaching and you're dead, Luciano."

At the words, he froze with his fingers just inside his jacket, while his arm quivered like it was a separate thing waiting for a signal. Luciano didn't want to stop reaching, and I knew it.

"You want it, Luciano," I said, shifting the .38 to the center of his chest. It was a personal hunting rule to keep any cutie like Luciano where you could hit home with the first shot. He was the sort of sweetheart that you don't gut shoot first for kicks because he'd stand there and take one through a soft place to get his own shot done. And maybe he'd still be standing there when he killed you. So you shot at the heavy bone areas like the chest where it would hit solid and knock him down.

The tossup on what it would be took some long seconds, before his arm sagged and relaxed without moving forward a hair. Normally, you could miss the small sag of an arm relaxing or the whisper of a breath being let out. I knew that Luciano was hearing my normal voice like I was shouting in his ear.

I said, "Take the gun out slow, Luciano. Don't blink, jerk it or drop it, and don't turn this way."

He followed orders closely, taking his gun out slowly. There was sweat on his face as he did it right. It was slow and easy, and the pistol reached the floor like a gambler putting down his last chip. I could hear his sigh when he stood up again.

"Walk away from it," I said, "to your right."

He stepped along the wall toward me. I let him put some distance between him and his gun before I said, "Now just turn around and lean against the wall." He leaned and froze while I got his gun, a wicked little .380 with a bone breaking slug and an eleven shot clip.

I emptied it and slapped the clip back in with a hollow click. "You make stupid mistakes, Luciano," I said. "Too bad you didn't try calling here first. You wouldn't have walked into it then."

I felt the weakness start in my legs again. It eats you up after any tension, and your legs feel limp for a bit. The feeling had got me slightly before Luciano had come, and I knew it damn sure was coming back now.

I walked up behind Luciano and swung his .380 in a clipping arc that crashed the blue steel solidly on the back of his skull. He grunted once on the way down. I made my legs get me to the nearest chair before they went twitchingly limp.

Watching Luciano, I had the uneasy feeling that things were coming too easy all of a sudden. I figured there had to be a catch to it, but you can't plan on making the right guess for all the moves in the game when it's a problem just to find out who is playing and on what side.

Maybe I wouldn't need to guess now since Luciano was a piece of the contract who should have all the answers.

My legs stopped shaking after awhile. I started feeling the way I had before, which wasn't good. I was bullet-holed, bruised, aching, and my nerves were like broken wires that quivered to the throb of my arm. But it was my turn to play for once because this time I had some answers. All I had to do was get them out of Luciano.

It took me awhile to get Luciano and Sandy tied into the hard-backed chairs I'd brought from the kitchen. When I finished, the twitching in my legs made me sit down quickly. The shaking lasted longer that time, and no part of it was fun. Looking at Luciano and Sandy in their chairs, I wondered how far I was from discovering how to fit Sandy and Luciano together.

CHAPTER THIRTEEN

I knew there was too much unfinished business and too many unanswered questions to consider the contract over. It was something to think about while I waited for Luciano and Sandy to wake up and join the land of reality again, so I could have a last try at making some sense out of what was going on. I realized very clearly that turning Luciano and Sandy over to Cardinalli should send me on my way with a satisfied customer behind me. There was only the problem of satisfying myself, because when your name is connected to a job that doesn't smell right, you stop getting jobs, and the bad word stays with you. I was sure, too, that Cardinalli wouldn't be any more cheerful about things when I did get there.

The way the job smelled, I decided to use the phone by the fireplace to call Kincaid at the motel. He was mad as hell and thin voiced with meanness, but three minutes later the phone clicked sharply in my ear, and I knew he was on his way to join the party.

I rubbed my eyes open and lit a cigarette before I went back across the room to Luciano and patted his face with a brisk, open handed slap that helped get him to pay attention and learn the facts.

"Well, sweetheart," I said, "has your safe and comfortable little world started to look like a shit hole now?" I grinned. "You up and coming punks usually don't see the shit until you go under, but you'll have a chance to enjoy going down in it if Cardinalli has any long range plans for you."

His face looked down. He was probably thinking about Cardinalli's plans. He was sure none of them would be fun. His features showed the strain. His eyes had too much hate showing in the look he threw at me. It was just hate, with no room for any deep gutted fear to show yet.

"You bastard," he said. "How did you do it?"

"A cop told me where you were," I said, knowing he wouldn't believe that.

Any distant hope that I'd get easy answers from Luciano faded as I read his eyes. You can't fake that look. It always gets in deep because of fear and anger. His eyes were black pools. Anything else was buried. He would take a lot before breaking. He was not looking forward to his visit with Cardinalli and kept that out of his mind with hate. I had to put it back in to get answers.

I wondered how long it would take to break him. I reminded myself he held the answers I had to have. He was the key to the contract stink and the answers that could fill the job in. I had to have them, and what I was thinking would have scared Luciano all right. He knew I didn't give a damn about how big he was or what I gave Cardinalli because I'd get my pay anyway.

I smiled at Luciano. There really wasn't a choice. He would talk because the decision was his life. He was a sure dead man in Cardinalli's hands. The answers I wanted were only tickets for making a clean contract.

Luciano's eyes said hate. He knew what the price was and that the limit on what I'd do was off. The room was quiet while we both thought it out and added the score. Luciano had his own answers first. He regarded me quietly. "Now, how does it go?" he asked finally. "Do you take me to Cardinalli?"

"Not right away. I've got questions you can answer first. You tell me the right answers, and you'll get to Cardinalli slower and in one piece. If I catch you lying, I'll work on you in pieces, and hamburger will look better than you, but I'll make you last a long time before Cardinalli gets what's left."

His mouth thinned. "You'll get something, too, when my boys get here. You'll get trouble then."

"Eddie and Carl have all they can handle, so don't scare me to death with men you only think you have."

"I don't know any Eddie or Carl."

I grinned and chopped the barrel of the .38 down on the thin bulge of his nose. I heard the bone snap. He choked back the scream as his eyes watered and blood spilled over his shirt front.

I waited until he met my eyes, then said, "That was a lie, Luciano. I told you they would cost you."

He managed a sneer and ignored me, looking down at the blood falling on his shirt, until I snapped his head up with a slap of the .38 and then smashed the barrel on his mouth.

He had trouble focusing his eyes, but I knew he could hear me. "We'll start the hard way, by making you toothless, Luciano. The girls won't like you so much then."

He shook his head to clear it while the thought worked at him. Luciano wasn't used to this sort of pressure. The fine art of working someone over was not so fine when you were catching instead of pitching. It wasn't so fine, either, if you had a good idea of what was coming because you had beat on a few heads yourself.

Maybe I could strip him down and break him very quickly with a knife, but if he did it himself and decided to talk rather than hurt, the answers he gave were more likely to be the truth. Another thing, I didn't care one hell of a lot for him either. He wasn't any prize nice fellow when he got racket big on death and fear and would've gotten bigger as he spread. So I wasn't going to feel all that bad about it if I had to tie him down and peel his hide off in small pieces to get what I wanted.

He managed to shake the fog out of his eyes and stare at me. The .38 had spoiled his jeer, too. It was hard to smirk or leer with split lips. I balanced the pistol for easier swinging.

"Now we got all that cleared up, haven't we? No lies, no smart remarks and no screwing around. I don't care how I give you to Cardinalli, baby. But we will have our conversation first, or it will be a long and unpleasant time for you." I smiled. "Cardinalli might treat you like a pain in the ass when he gets you. He might even bury you deep. What I'll do is things you can avoid with a few answers. Make it easy on yourself, Luciano. I'm going to get the answers I want anyway."

His eyes didn't change but his face twitched when he thought about Cardinalli and reaching the place where he would do his dying. He wanted to ignore that until the moment arrived, and maybe he wanted to keep a little hope of not having to do one of Cardinalli's vanishing acts in the river.

He had a tight look of fear on his face. The wash of hate from his eyes didn't keep him from realizing that I was his last stop before he got Cardinalli and the river.

His fixed stare on my face wavered and fell to watching his nose drip red on his shirt front. I reached out casually and chopped the barrel of the .38 across his nose and got a quick gasp of pain along with his full attention.

I grinned bleakly. "You either play the question game, or I'll make you play it. But you don't pull in your head like you can sit in the middle."

Luciano's voice had thickened with the smashed nose. "What do you want answers for when you already got us? You found answers to get here, so you got it all."

"I want everything in a neat package with no loose ends."

He shook his head. "How should I know what you found out to get here? Go ask Cardinalli what you don't know."

I put a welt on his head with the .38 again and had him jerking quickly every time I wagged it at him.

"You're getting a nice collection of lumps, baby. Now, you keep your mouth shut and pay attention. I'll tell you how I figure it went, and you fill in any holes there are. If I get part of it wrong, you tell me where. You make it sound right, or I start taking your teeth out with this gun."

He waited a moment, then nodded. I dug a photo out of my pocket and held it where he could study it. It was Billy Swan's photo of Luciano and Sandy together.

"Your mistake, Luciano, the one Cardinalli hadn't seen."

He twisted his head and looked at Sandy. "The little bastard always took pictures you didn't know about," he said.

"That was really the tip-off, but it didn't fit until later. We should do a rundown of your last two years, Luciano. You did some very select bits of jockeying around and almost made it to the top of the pile before you blew it. Let's start with Sandy here. Seeing her with Billy Swan was the ticket to bigtime you were looking for, wasn't it? Shouldn't have had any trouble cutting Swan out either and having her park her shoes under your bed. Then it was just a matter of getting her strung out enough to start getting some handy tips for you about Cardinalli's action. Maybe she got her kicks from giving dear old dad a screwing, and you started being right on every takeover you tried after that. But why not, when you knew what part of his rackets were weak before he could patch them up. Sandy wouldn't have any problem in getting that sort of information. She likely had the thoughtful daughter act in the city. You took a big chunk out of Cardinalli's rackets in those small pieces, thanks to her. It was bigtime, like you wanted, and it came easy because a person like Cardinalli wouldn't believe his own blood was giving him the screwing, even if you told him about it. You'd have to shove his name and tradition down his throat before he'd believe Sandy would do it. All of that gave you easy going and a name for being the up-and-coming punk around town."

I paused and gave him a chance to change or add anything while I sorted out my guess at the rest.

"That part is almost a sure bet, Luciano. But I have to guess some from there on, so pay attention and be helpful, or you get some .38 therapy. You could have piece-worked Cardinalli to death with your set-up by playing it careful. Like taking over enough to grow on but never a big enough grab to give him a bad scare so that he'd call in voting hands of other cities. You'd have thought the local talent had been playing when a few teams of other cities came in on your ass.

"But maybe you take stupid pills or went and got greedy and pushed too far. You had to know that Cardinalli would have let the small chunks go because calling in help is saying he can't handle it, and maybe a new boss would get put in. I think you got to feeling too damn big and wanted to get a big enough piece of him in one hack that would put you on top. Greedy enough, at least, to forget Cardinalli couldn't cover a big loss and would have to take a counsel vote.

"It was too big for one man, Luciano, but tell me why you needed to stop a good thing like bleeding

Cardinalli and to give the whole Mafia a reason to take a chunk out of your ass?" I shook my head at him. "I'm eager to hear the reasoning you used there, so go ahead and wise me up."

He glared at me for a long time, like he had to decide between a lie or a bluff and knew the risk on either one. "It's your fun today, Judas," he muttered. "Don't forget to remember me on your turn when someone takes you apart. It's loose but right, like you got it so far. But he got worried and nervous enough to start talking about outside talent like you. A big piece out of him would have done it. I thought he'd pay for Sandy."

"Okay, maybe he would have, but Pappas would have known, so he had to ask for a vote, and the whole game was wasted. You were feeling too sure of yourself when you set up a kidnap that even a rookie cop wouldn't buy. But maybe you figured he'd pay, and then you could let him see her on your side." I grinned at the silent girl. "You two make a good team, Luciano. She sat it out all morning for a chance to shoot me. If she hadn't lied about knowing you when I had that picture in my pocket, she might have made it. I added your boys in then as her bodyguards, and I knew why they were careless. They didn't have to watch her, and they figured the lodge was safe. It made sense, then, why a team of old pros were so sloppy."

I lit a cigarette and grinned bleakly at him. "You might have been smart enough to worry about a slip when you knew I was on you. So you tried to tidy things up until you got the payoff. Swan got hit then, and you put Potts and Bello out on me while you tried to get the deal over. The slip was driving Cardinalli over the line where he got told to let you have Sandy. He'd keep that Mafia code he likes so much. The choice won't improve your health, Luciano. You just grabbed a bigger piece than you could handle, baby. That's the rundown on the rise and fall of Luciano, from the outside view. It's your turn to make noise now. You should find it easy to tidy up all my mistakes by remembering there's not one reason I know of for not pounding on you and enjoying it until your tired ass is worn out." I grinned. "All I need is a lie or so to remember how hard you worked at trying to kill me."

Luciano spent a long moment staring at Sandy before he shrugged and said, "What do you want, bastard? You got the story right, and you got us. So you're winners all the way around." He paused, then added, "Should we sit here and tell you how smart you were to get lucky?"

I wagged the .38 at him. "You got some slack on your ass right now, Luciano. That wise mouth will get it snugged up fast."

He shrugged. "There's nothing to tell you. Maybe you guessed better than you thought." There was a weird smirk on his face for a moment. "Cardinalli couldn't come up with a better one to give you."

I thought it over and lit another cigarette, while the silence grew in the room. The placid acceptance I was getting didn't fit. There was an ugly docility to it, like they knew something I didn't and were all too eager to let me keep the answers I had. You could call it a reasonable bet when you knew that there was no place to go with questions after someone gave you an answer. I didn't push it because I knew I had everything my guessing would get me. There wasn't any satisfaction in the answer I had. The idea that there was a better one played on my nerves in the increasing silence.

I tried to shake the idea off, along with the thought that I could be missing the place where the stink was. There were too many places in the contract maze that a new answer could be. I couldn't take this one to Luciano because I didn't have the right questions to ask, along with the .38 therapy, or a place to start any guessing.

Luciano and Sandy watched me from across the

room when I tried the run again. Their blank expressions seemed to make what answer pieces I did have scatter like a dropped dish.

I watched myself in the mirror behind the small bar and felt the fatigue that showed in the shadowed face of my reflection. It made me want an end to it and a quick way out that didn't include my dying.

The lodge had an unreal feeling in the unusual silence, one that didn't belong with three people in a room. I shook my head, feeling like a punch-drunk fighter who had won the main event but was somehow getting the hell beat out of him in sparring practice. I had bodies to deliver, my money to collect and an answer for the contract. It should have been enough, but when you added it all up, there wasn't any answer.

It seemed like a long time before I heard the sound of Kincaid's rented car. It was Kincaid who brought the answers I needed, along with a clear, cold dose of reality that cleared up the maze and contract question.

It wasn't what I expected from Kincaid. I expected the usual thing, like the fact that he might be unhappy over not being in on the fun part of the night, but you could bet an activity like spooking around in a dark lodge with Kincaid and a gun wasn't on my list of things to do. So he could stay unhappy. I also expected to see his jaw drop open like a dead fish when I told him that saving young girls for Cardinalli when they didn't want to be saved could be very tacky. In all, I expected a lot and didn't think about Kincaid being too pro, just one who was better than most.

I figured I didn't need to beat him at anything when I opened the door to surprise him with some bits of wisdom. My .38 was a world away under my arm, while I nodded toward Luciano and Sandy.

But Kincaid already knew what it was all about and had more of the facts than I did. He knew he was there on a job and that was all he needed to know to keep it from showing on his face, while the door was still closing. I caught the look of kill too late and was still turned half away when a gun appeared in his hand, and a blur of quick hardness cracked solidly into the side of my head. The blow, along with the surprise of being on my knees, made the four rapid shots sound vague, like the shooting was being done in another room.

It was Kincaid's type of murder, with second, make sure shots on each hit. Maybe he'd add a few more for kicks. It was how you dealt it to another hired gun or racket pro, what was called a double-kill. It was getting used as kicks by a son-of-a-bitch who'd practiced on safe and tied targets.

My legs wouldn't work, my mind was getting weary pictures which wouldn't register completely during the shooting, but the reality of it was clear, slamming into my mind as I saw the puppet-like jerks Luciano and Sandy made under the impact of hot lead, as their chairs toppled over. I didn't need to see the dark stain spreading around the bullet holes to get the answers loud and clear. But answers don't help when you get them like an echo that is too late in coming.

CHAPTER FOURTEEN

Maybe under normal conditions I would have been ready for Kincaid, and it wouldn't have been a free turkey-shoot. But there hadn't been anything normal about the contract since it started. I watched Kincaid's thumb on the hammer of his .38 and listened to his breath hiss out over his tight lips.

"Now you get how you finish this contract, Judas. I got to go back and tell about the good work you do."

The weight of my .38 kept reminding me it was too far. I was getting the same choice I'd handed Luciano earlier. A fast, clean slug for trying for my gun, or I could let myself hope Kincaid might slip some before he decided to pull the trigger.

"You moved sooner than I expected, Kincaid," I said.

His eyes were still eager with getting his kicks. He was enjoying his work when I handed him a curve. He was the winner of a cute game, and I wanted to chip a piece off it with a small unexpected thing that would maybe make his trigger finger relax and stop squeezing. I knew it was buying seconds with a long shot, but the .38 didn't go off. Instead, a question came into his eyes. He hated me just enough not to want me to be right on anything when he finished it. He gave a laugh that came out thin and high. There was nothing funny about it. "Sooner than *you* figured, Judas?" he said. "You didn't come close to figuring it out, or I wouldn't be here. I knew you didn't have it when I let you back me down at the motel."

I tried to grin. "You *let* me back you down, Kincaid? Or was it just that you ran out of guts when it got to taking a chance on dying?"

He didn't like it at all, but his gun never moved off the center of my chest.

"You're a smart bastard, ain't you?" His mouth pulled into a thin smile. "That crap you laid on Cardinalli about the outfit's rules fits you pretty good. You got your own lousy rules. I never had to worry about getting it in the back from you, see? But you had to worry about me, didn't you? No rules, Judas. That's what comes out winning."

"How long does it win, Kincaid? Until somebody gets scared of it and has you iced?"

The smile left him then. "Get off it, Judas. You got picked to get burned, I didn't." He paused to tilt the gun up until it was pointed at my face. "Unless you want to call this a payoff."

"Maybe that's what Pappas and Cardinalli intended to pay you with, too. One more double-cross shouldn't bother any."

"Just lose that idea, bastard," he said. "They need me, like they needed me for this job, because they knew you wouldn't kill the bitch for selling Cardinalli out. She had to go, or there would have been a new boss. You got to play at finding her for me. A lot of planning went into how to use you. Pappas and Cardinalli's work.

"Which one has plans for you, punk?"

That got me the gun once across the face, again with enough steam to stagger me and slit the flesh over my cheekbone. Kincaid was watching the blood track down my face and nodding slowly when I shook my head clear. The smile he had then was pure pleasure. The day was full of kicks for him. It made me wonder if buying time off a trigger squeeze hadn't gotten me a higher price on the waiting time. The sort of entertainment Kincaid liked to use to tick away the minutes wouldn't agree with me at all.

He kept his smile, watching me like he'd found a new toy, before he said, "You're going to tell me you're scared, Judas. I want to remember you like that. Just like you'll think I'd be doing you a damn favor to pull this trigger."

"That's something you can't get, punk," I said, although my guts started knotting like coiled snakes.

"I'll get it, all right." He lifted his .38 until I could look into the bore. "Get rid of your gun."

You make a choice like that reluctantly. There was that minute for a try, to find a chance, but no one checks in early. I shed my own .38 slowly and carefully stood up after he had kicked it away.

"Start thinking about dying, Judas," he said. "You're doing it by seconds right now. I'm the one thing that lets you keep breathing." He paused and licked his lips. "You'll want to quit doing it in awhile."

With Kincaid you would believe it. I knew where my limit was so I shrugged it off. "Nobody dreams as big as a punk," I said, wondering how much emptiness he could hear in my words.

"I'm glad you think it's a dream, Judas." He laughed again. "A real hard-ass should make it take longer. Pappas will like knowing how long it took to finish you exactly like he said."

I watched his smile.

"You want to know what he said, Judas?" he asked.

"He didn't even know he was talking and telling me exactly how to make the hit."

"He probably tells you how to wipe your ass, too."

Kincaid smiled nicely. "He said to burn you, that's all. But I'm really going to burn you, bastard, and not with just a bullet."

"You figure I'll do it myself with matches or something?"

"You'll do just what I say. Or else I get to shoot off both your kneecaps and do it myself. You're dead, you know. Now start walking outside—real slow."

I could feel the sudden sweat on my face as we moved outside. I knew it stank of fear. I knew also that Kincaid was past just a sadistic nature and was as crazy a son-of-a-bitch as you'd find, but you didn't doubt he'd do what he said. I could feel myself tightening up while he walked grinning behind me. The slim chances left to play were running out with time.

Kincaid's jolly anticipation of the coming event didn't show in the .38 aimed at me. He kept it close to him, trained on me, and he didn't get sloppy with the perfect day's record he had so far. It was played tight and close out to the garage, where I picked up a can of fuel oil he'd found. His eyes were bright, and his laugh was a high-pitched giggle as he watched me.

"That's nice," he said. "You sure look good carrying your own way to burn. This is worth more than they could pay me."

His eyes seemed almost glossy when he talked, but he didn't let what he was feeling make him a bit careless because he knew the price there would be to pay.

The schedule called for a well cooked corpse for him to enjoy. I was going to be it unless I could hand him something he didn't expect. I could feel the sun's heat on my back while I looked at the lake and the distant resorts.

"You don't get to play here, Kincaid. People might wonder what you're burning." His glance swept the lake and back to me. "Smart bastard," he said. "We'll go around in the back then. You can start begging anytime, but you still burn."

The keyed up sound of his voice made me careful. It wouldn't take much for a move of any kind to get a slug through the leg. As long as he kept thinking about his fire, he wouldn't be looking at anything else but me. I hoped there was a surprise around for Kincaid yet.

I kept my eyes on the woodline as I walked to the back of the lodge. What I wanted to see would be there in the wall of bush and evergreen. I sorted through the fatigue and shaky nerve inside me for the exact words that had set up a cure for other possible problems at the lodge. If Butcher was aware of my predicament it could give Kincaid a trip to the morgue.

There had been no doubt at all that the lodge and upcoming problems were a possibility when Butcher and I had talked it out. We had added Butcher's old sniper talents as a handy bit of aid for my visit. His rifle there was my surprise way out if I had to leave in a hurry. It had been a way out, at least, before the players switched partners. Butcher's effectiveness would be no help at all if he did not see Kincaid as a problem to be buried. Any way you took it, you couldn't put a whole hell of a lot of hope on Butcher's knowing our simple, little plan had been given a new twist. In all truth, it was very possible that Butcher was nowhere near the back door, the lodge or Smokey Lake, for that matter. Our nicely laid plan had called for my arrival that morning, so my night spooking would be another twist, another reason for Butcher to pack up promptly and travel when I didn't appear.

You didn't need to tell yourself to bet all your chips on any spider-web thin hope under these circumstances. I studied the woodline like I'd just discovered nature. The blank expanse of green and shadows looked as empty as the pockets of a jack-rolled drunk.

I had a few choice names for the stupidity of not finding Butcher first. At second best, I would have followed our plan and got to the lodge at the right time. It didn't help one bit to have some reasons for mistakes when you were close to dying. I threw a last look at the woods. Even if Butcher was out there, my showing up with Kincaid would make him wonder. Maybe he'd hesitate too long.

Suddenly behind me Kincaid laughed. I didn't want to know what had crawled across his mind and tickled him. You could keep a little hope right down to the line, but it's easier to let it go and find some other way to help you get ready for dying. If you can hate enough, it gets easier, too. I wanted more than anything to get Kincaid's neck in my hands and make things do the tiny popping and snapping when I squeezed.

There was one thing he had said which he couldn't risk doing because it could be a mistake which would kill him. His leg shooting promise was valid if he shot a leg out from under me any time before I tried him. That's where the sport ended. He would have maybe two shots to keep me off him then. You don't waste those on trying for a leg.

He was walking carefully with the anticipation of death in his eyes. He kept me where his .38 had me covered.

"That's far enough," he said. "No one's going to see you back here."

I turned to face him in the clearing. This might have been as good as any time could be, but the gun was tight in his hand. He was waiting for it because I couldn't cover the way I'd tightened up.

His eyes slid over me. "You know something, bastard?" he grinned. "You're still thinking of a way out. You ain't scared enough."

"Being scared wouldn't change anything, would it, punk?"

"Sure," he said. "You beg real good and you buy

time at living. But you don't buy much, Judas. This isn't your day."

I got a jerked laugh out and let him read what I was going to do in my face. "You'll have to do it the hard way, punk. No fire for fun because you'll have to shoot at more than my leg to keep me off you."

The gun steadied and froze, pointed at my chest. "We can do it that way, too, Judas," he said.

The time was gone then. He knew that I'd come as far as the .38 could push me and that I'd try for him no matter what he did. He didn't like that slim risk of my getting my hands on him. I watched his eyes narrow to thin slits. His expression said it was all over as he started to squeeze the trigger.

That was enough warning to let me start for him and then to know it was too far. It was six steps. The .38 at the end of it made the distance a long trip to nowhere and all one way. The sound of his gun with the impact of lead was all I expected. The snap sound of a slug going by, real close didn't register until I saw Kincaid jerk backward to the wet sound of his .38 blasting into the earth between us. It was the last shot he ever triggered. The next two slugs snapped past me and slammed him backward with leaden echo of smashed flesh and bone.

His face was a study in surprise. He didn't believe he was dying, even while his shirt bloomed with red splashes around the bullet holes. His legs kept carrying him backward for a few steps after the last slug, until he crumpled like old rags, with his eyes open to the sun.

The sudden silence then was the sort you wait in, as though the scene had frozen. I realized I was waiting for the deep report of the rifle behind the slug Kincaid had caught. There was no doubt in my mind then about the speed and effectiveness of the Butcher's rifle work, and I knew he'd used a silencer as the final assurance his shooting position wouldn't be picked out.

That combination was the vicious snap of a near miss. You didn't hear the slug that got you so you could be surprised as hell over getting hit. I walked over to Kincaid to check.

He was on the way then. Death sagged his features. His chest a pulp under three holes which you could cover with your hand. The mess was a kind that only big, soft-nose slugs from a rifle can make. His eyes had almost lost their brightness when I stood over him.

I didn't want him to die easy. I smiled down at him, saying, "You waited too long, punk. And you got a day of kicks. But I get to use the fuel oil, now."

He jerked his eyes open. His mouth only leaked red when he tried to talk. The last thing he did was stare at my smile.

I sat down beside him because my legs felt shaky and my guts crawled. I watched Butcher make his way across the clearing toward me. I shivered in the sun from the fear I'd held back. I wondered how thin the line had been between living and dying. Butcher had shaved it very fine.

I could feel pain in my slug-torn arm now, a deep, steady throb, with the nerves quivering like broken wires.

Cardinalli had wanted the problem of his daughter solved, but he wanted her removed, not returned to him. They had known I wouldn't touch that sort of kill and had used me to locate her for Kincaid, who couldn't find anything but always was eager to murder. He had also gotten a kill order on me because they didn't want me coming back unhappy over the use they had put the available talent to. They didn't want me there to call it a double-cross later when I could hurt them.

The past days had left me looking for a place to hang a hate on, and the double-cross gave me the answer of where to put it. I could find a little eagerness for the contract now. It was my turn to play with all the pieces—things like Kincaid had been paid in full. But Kincaid's death did not even the score when my contract payment had been scheduled as a slug and a shallow grave.

It was an unhappy fact that sometimes the ones who hired you considered talk about the job later as dangerous to them. It followed that they would have a passing thought on the merits of a hot lead payoff. You learned the rules to survive on contracts until it hit the place where you got the only retirement plan there was. To survive, you didn't leave a deal like Sandy Cardinalli connected to your name. Her death was connected to me now in such a way that there wouldn't be a peep about Kincaid when the word spread.

There was a high price on dealing a double-cross on this job. I know Cardinalli had a heavy bill due. The surprise of delivering it to him would be interesting. Having the wrong man come back to collect was going to really worry and surprise him.

I looked up from my seat beside Kincaid. Butcher was there with a meaningless smile on his face and a look in his eyes I'd seen before. It's the deep, sick look behind a kill that some men never get dug out, no matter how many times the trigger is pulled.

The rifle he carried was a one job gun, with a scope and silencer you didn't need on game. The caliber was a big bastard, 8mm, that used 200 grains of lead to do a job with no nonsense. You didn't get up with holes from that rifle in you.

Butcher waited me out until I sat up and said, "You got to have a lot of bastard in you, Butcher. There was damn little time left when you shot."

He nodded at the body. "I knew he wasn't taking you target shooting when I saw his gun. But from the time you came around that corner until I did shoot, you managed to keep your dead ass in between us. I could have hit him all right; all I had to do was go through you first."

I managed a tired grin. "No bitch coming from here then." I shivered some with a cold chill and looked at Kincaid. "He could have been the one I kept expecting, Butcher, because he had me anytime he wanted to try. I couldn't beat him. Kincaid picked the one place he couldn't win at, like luck wore out for him first."

Butcher shrugged. "It did wear out, didn't it? Like yours will when you hit the right one." He nodded at his handiwork. "Somebody always pulls your card when the time comes."

He looked at the body and then away. "This one's Kincaid, I suppose?" he asked. "You know he's a contract man, right?"

"I know he damn near added me to the score he has. Yeah, he's a murder-by-trade boy. Why? Did you expect him to be a trained ape?"

Butcher let it go for a little while and kept looking at his work. "I know what to expect, Judas," he said. "I wanted to be sure the right one got it."

"Yeah, well, he was the right one when he pointed that gun at me, buddy. That's all you need to know to kill someone. That walk we were taking wasn't any field trip. Those aren't in the Mafia's list of events."

I was close to asking him if he needed a contract man's union card out of Kincaid's wallet or something, but I kept it back. I knew he was only rationalizing his killing. If there were other reasons for shooting, he didn't need to admit that revenge was sweet and the biggest reason he was there.

Butcher was watching me silently. A questioning expression pushed out the sick look which his face had held. He nodded toward the lodge.

"How about the girl, Judas?"

It was an answer that he'd already paid the going rate for, I admitted. But there were several things I'd rather do than pass out answers that proved the contract was hung around my neck like a dead fish and that I hadn't found the stink in it. It didn't help that he'd come along like a seagull after a fish boat, either.

I shook my head at him and said the talk came later. I sent him after the Ford. Then I rearranged the bandages on my arm while I waited with Kincaid. I had no urge to wait in the lodge. I wondered how Butcher would like the full odor of it?

It was going to be a tacky bit of business to explain the whole thing to Butcher, when the name of the game seemed to be double-cross and the last man standing got the chips.

You had to admit it would take a trusting fellow not to wonder if some hanky-panky and a screwing had been given you. Butcher, now, was not an overly trusting guy. He was an ex-cop who had a few years at doubting any story he heard. It was going to be a little hard to explain Luciano's trip to big time, Sandy's wayward ways and Cardinalli's bit of Mafia revenge.

There wasn't an easy way to get all the facts out, when the unpleasant fact was that we had started a job and you couldn't call what was in the lodge a big success. Butcher might start calling it a success at the same time that he decided the screwed feeling he had was handed out by me.

It was going to be a tough and bitter pill to swallow. I didn't know how Butcher would take it yet. I had an urge to get back to the city where there was a bill to collect and a surprise to deliver into Cardinalli's grubby little hands.

CHAPTER FIFTEEN

Something or someone, some bastard like Butcher, always seems to come along and break the rules of the trade. They just come along and walk into your world, making a personal problem when you can't afford to be involved in any. You learn to work at not getting involved like it was a major part of staying alive, and it is. Then someone gets over the well honed edge that you keep between yourself and the human race.

I resented hell out of owing Butcher one damn big favor. It gave me something to think about while I sat outside the lodge and watched the flies starting to pay a working interest in Kincaid. I didn't like to owe a thing. It's all well and good that everybody may owe a favor or a bill somewhere, but mine is a cash trade, and it's habit to owe no bills.

The simple reason that I didn't want to owe Butcher a favor was that it might slow me down when old man death swung his reaper. That's one game which you play nimble and best alone. While you could drink a toast to an old gun buddy who had gone under, you made damn sure you didn't go with him. You'll get one thing besides dead from dying for a friend, and that is a live friend who might wonder at times what sort of stupid ass you'd been.

In no case did I need Butcher along as a portable problem, either. Only, Butcher had paid his dues to see this job out, and the debt was there. The rules and regulations of the racket subculture dictated how I could pay Butcher back. My business was no place for the squeamish. Those rules suggested that a problem like Butcher be removed. Even after I knew what I had to do with him, I wondered how any problems could really be solved this way, but I guessed that in a world where you can get crippled by a very nice guy, you couldn't expect a hell of a lot of favors and play from a contract man.

So what in hell did I owe Butcher, anyway? I asked myself. Besides saving me from being the main attraction at Kincaid's body burning, it was all his idea. He'd asked to come along, hadn't he? His hate was as much reason as he needed to pull that trigger. He even got his pound of flesh in revenge and maybe a gold star for shooting a badman.

The favor I owed him was a big one, I'll admit, but I didn't owe him anything else. It wasn't my place to come up with a cover story because the contract was a stacked deck, and we had gone ahead with the play. Since it was his choice to come along to play in the shit pile, he had to stay there like the rest of us. I hadn't planned the stink into the contract.

So to hell with it.

I dealt the same load of crap to Butcher when he came back with the car and we took in the view inside the lodge. I kept it short, all right, but he got all the high points of the game. I rubbed the facts in deep, right from all our wasted leg work to the fine point of fifteen minutes earlier when he did his thing with the rifle.

Then I let him roll it around a few times to come up with some questions and things to think about. It made Butcher think about bastards, and he settled for me since I was handy. I couldn't say it was the worst moment of my life. I've spent worse over being the cause of dying to men I've worked with. It happens. But Butcher had trusted me to put the right man in front of his gun at the right time and putting the right one there at the wrong time wasn't enough.

In the stillness of the lodge, I could see Butcher thinking while he looked at Sandy. He was figuring that since the old double-cross had been worked, there was not much assurance that he had not gotten one, too. His eyes asked me if the job hadn't worked out exactly like I wanted, with him at the end to play chump. I didn't blame him.

I walked over to start untying Sandy. Butcher watched like he didn't care for that at all. I wasn't crazy about it, either.

While I worked at the knots, I listened to Butcher's movements behind me. I figured he wouldn't use the gun because he'd want one bastard to give Thierney. For once I figured it right.

It worked nice, too. He covered the last few feet of carpet between us with fast steps and tried to bring his sniper rifle into use as a club. Staying on my knees, I twisted around enough to flick the thin blade of my knife out and let him walk right up the sharp blade which I held low.

I needed all my attention on where the blade went in. Butcher damn near brained me with the rifle before he felt the steel in his guts and let the rifle go to grab what he expected to be a Potts type of gutting. I came up with the blade pulled out, hoping that it was over.

Butcher looked like he was worried about other things than me. He kept both hands over the hole in his guts, without wasting time to go under his shirt for a closer look.

There was plenty of blood, I saw, but if he was put together like everyone else inside, he had only a tidy little hole, which could scare hell out of a man because of the blood and steady pain.

Butcher had added me to his list of people to hate when he looked up. However, I was none too popular with him when he tried to club me with the rifle, either.

I put him through the search routine and patted him down before I tossed his rifle out of reach and returned to finish the job of untying Sandy's body. It took a little while and a set of drapes from the lodge for a body shroud before she was wrapped for a trip.

I looked at Butcher. "You would have starved to death as a cop, Butcher. Your face told it like you'd picked me for the goat in this, and your lousy shoes squeak no matter what you walk on."

He stood there and hurt in silence, holding his stomach like he was having a hernia attack.

"Were you going to feed me to Thierney so you could be sure you hadn't gotten a double-cross?"

His voice sounded dull. "You knew what the contract was," he said. "You couldn't have walked into this blind."

"I knew what *my* contract was, Butcher. Not what Kincaid's covered or what Cardinalli really wanted."

"Yeah. So you just let Kincaid walk in and go to work."

I let it go. To hell with explaining it. He looked worried about opening up like a wet sack, and he wasn't going to believe anything I had to say about how he got that way.

I shook my head at him and picked up the girl's body. "Believe what you want," I told him. "Now get out and get in the car."

His expression said that he knew his guts would fall out if he tried to move, but he got going carefully. It was slow work getting the body in the back seat and him in the front.

His voice sounded thin. "What happens next?"

"Next, baby, you'd better clamp your jaws together because it's a long, hard haul to Chicago." I paused a moment. "You started this by trying to brain me, Butcher, so I'm delivering the girl to Cardinalli before I let you get to Thierney and arrange a cell for me."

He jerked his head toward the back seat. "Why drive her back to Chicago?"

"Honey, baby," I said and gave him a tired grin, "she's what Cardinalli paid for in the long run, so he'll get her."

"You deliver like he wants," he said softly, "and he wanted her dead."

"I deliver what he pays on."

His expression kept me on his list as number one bastard, but I didn't have the energy to put the double-cross where it belonged. All I wanted was for him to stay put until I was finished and could put some distance between myself and Thierney, who wasn't likely to ask questions at all about how my knife had made a hole in Butcher's stomach. He was just narrow minded enough to shoot me before any talking started.

It was likely that Butcher, too, would take a long time at getting around to thinking I'd done him a favor. But he'd start thinking about it when some doc told him that his belly hole was in the right spot for saving his guts. He'd remember things like I could have stopped him even easier with my .38.

It was a long way back to Chicago. We met rain outside the city. Butcher's face had a gray-white color. I took the chance of calling Thierney.

I didn't let Thierney talk any while I told him what Butcher would need when he got to him, but he said what he wanted to say before I could hang up. With Thierney, the message wasn't at all hard to understand, when he figured me to be about as clean as a Maxwell

Street alley. His sanitation project seemed to consist of me in the morgue. It gave me lots of reasons to keep some distance between us and to keep my stay short while I collected the contract payment. A long visit to Cardinalli wasn't in my plans anyway.

In town, I finally ran into some good luck. The rain had emptied the streets, and Cardinalli's Cad had the parking zone in front of his office building all to itself. There was only Butcher's hate to share the night with, while I moved Sandy's body to the Cad. I spent ten minutes at sweating before I was finished.

I moved the Ford back and parked a block away, while I thought about having to pass on my surprise to Cardinalli. As I got out of the car, Butcher said he'd hope doing it would kill me. It was a cheerful thought to take up in the elevator.

CHAPTER SIXTEEN

The days hadn't changed Cardinalli's office any, but it seemed like I'd been away a long time when the smell of his cigars reminded me of working up there on the contract night. You could count the days in hours all right, but when you counted time in bodies, you could grow old fast.

I didn't bother to knock politely when I let myself into the office. The slack jaw expression that Cardinalli and Pappas had when they saw me was pure surprise. Whatever they expected, it wasn't me. I enjoyed the surprise, while I stood there and felt a thousand years old.

It was almost a minute before fear edged into their faces. They had reason to worry when they saw their plans fall apart like wet toilet paper. Cardinalli grew beads of sweat on his face. Pappas gripped the arms of his chair like he was trying to strangle it. They had to grab for straws, wondering how much I knew and why I'd spoiled their cheerful evening by being alive. They would have to play it cute and cozy now, just like screwing the hired hand hadn't been in their schedule at all.

I stretched the silence I'd brought into the room to a wire's edge before I grinned for them. I nodded to Pappas. "Your boy didn't make it. He's out in the boondocks doing his bit for nature by feeding the flies and making a bad smell."

They exchanged a quick glance. Cardinalli got his cigar out of his mouth to ask, "What happened, Judas? You were working together, weren't you?"

"Oh, we worked like hell together," I grinned. "Real team work. Like I worked and he watched until payday came and he wanted all the goodies. Then we didn't work so fine together any more."

"Did you kill him, or where's he at?" Pappas wanted to know.

"Let's say he died from an overdose of my stupid pill. That north woods air is hell on the lungs when there's lead in it." I shook a cigarette out and lit it, enjoying the feeling of having the answers for a change.

"But he did take care of just about everything before he went. Like Luciano. Now there's a problem that ain't around any more. Kincaid was an effective son-of-a-bitch right to the end."

I let them worry it out and waited like a stone until Cardinalli licked his lips and got it asked.

"The girl," he said softly. "Was she with him?"

I took the picture of Luciano and Sandy out of my jacket and dropped it on his desk. "Just like that, Cardinalli. They had some togetherness going which they liked so much that they even had some boys around to discourage idiots like me who thought she needed to be sprung. She didn't want any part of coming home to papa."

They sweated nicely from that. I wagged my head at Cardinalli.

"That was the sort of cute little game I told you not

to play. You could've kept it as a friendly little kill contract for the pair instead of sending me out on that kidnap crap." I shrugged. "We could have had nice, clean business then."

Cardinalli glanced at Pappas, then asked, "You would have taken a contract on her?"

"What are we, Cardinalli, choir boys? Do you think I give a damn who goes, so long as I get paid?" I grinned, "I'd hit your mother if the price was right."

They liked it better then. Dying must have seemed farther away. Cardinalli even tried a weak chuckle.

"We all make mistakes, Judas. You know how it goes. That fool Kincaid had us believing you wouldn't take a hit for a woman. But we needed you to find her."

"And Kincaid for the shooting, huh?"

"Something like that," Cardinalli said. "We were sure he'd get her if the chance came up." He rubbed his hands together. "We'll add a little extra to your contract for that mistake, of course."

I would have enjoyed telling him a little extra wouldn't quite cover his mistake of Kincaid's orders to kill me, but I stayed busy at keeping my grin for the big understanding we were having.

Cardinalli was still eager for news on his touchy subject. Though he reluctantly realized that he might never learn all the details for his second-hand enjoyment, he had to try.

"So you know all of it, then," he said. "What happened to that bitch daughter of mine; you didn't say?"

"No, I didn't, did I? But let's talk about money first, Cardinalli. I always remember better on a full wallet."

You could bury Cardinalli in money until he died under the load but he'd always be hungry enough to keep yelling for one more shovelful. I was getting him where it hurt, in the wallet. He wanted to know how to avoid paying, but he wanted the news more. He took the money from a wall safe and counted out five thousand for the contract. Then, seeing my unhappy expression, he started counting out the mistake money. I let him slow count the second pile until it was two more thousand, before I grinned and told him mistakes came high.

You could call them impatient when I counted the payoff one more time before putting it into my jacket pocket. Cash healed all, according to their thinking. Maybe it did, but I still had a tender spot to get patched up.

"Well, what happened to her?" Cardinalli asked, when we were all grinning again.

"Just what was supposed to happen," I said. "She is another problem you don't have running around now."

Pappas sighed. "Wait a minute. How can we be sure we got what you've been paid for? We don't know what kind of information she could have. How do we know?"

"Because I say so," I grinned. "But after seeing the cute games you people play, I figured you might not trust me, so I brought a surprise back for you."

They watched me and waited.

"Your daughter, Cardinalli," I said. "She's all gift-wrapped and dead as hell for you. She's down in the back seat of your car."

I nodded at them. "You can be sure she's dead when you bury her. I wouldn't have her lying around too long, if I were you. I hope the work will help you remember not to play cute games on a contract."

They managed to get out a few pet names for me as I left. I hadn't expected them to be happy with a body. I smiled all the way back to the car and Butcher.

"What's the price of bodies today, ghost?" he asked. "Or do those come free with the double-cross?"

There isn't a hell of a lot a man can believe after you stick a knife in his guts. I decided that a talk wasn't worth the effort and that however he decided now wouldn't change things one bit.

"The price of bodies is always high, Butcher," I told him. "I just sold one in a surprise package. Nothing gets tossed in free in this racket."

He coughed and held his guts tighter. "You get what you sell yourself for," he said. "So dump me out for Thierney. I'm tired of your smell."

"Shut up," I said. "Just shut up until you work your mind before you run your mouth. I'm tired of that off key song, and you're looking more like a half finished job every time I see you."

He shut up.

As I waited with Butcher, I listened to the rain play its snare drum march on the roof of the car. I knew my ache-filled tiredness wanted some bottled in bond, one hundred proof escape, but there was one thing out there in the night I wanted to see. It seemed like a long time before Cardinalli and Pappas came out of the building to check on the dirt I'd left them. I felt an empty sort of expectation like I was seeing a re-run of a movie, only the scene I was watching had a one time showing and was dim behind the wetness of the windshield.

Butcher caught my tenseness and forgot that his guts hurt. I didn't expect any nod from him or Thierney. The rackets were one place where nobody really took anything without someone thinking about the day they paid for it.

Cardinalli and Pappas appeared to be unhappy in the rain with the surprise package they were discovering.

The two minutes they spent before getting into the car seemed a timeless limbo until the gray wetness of the rain shattered in the red whoosh and white flash bloom of high octane combined with five sticks of dynamite. Bello's old booby trap for me made the place where the Cad had been into a spreading fire-ball of cooked meat and twisted metal.

I thought there must have been a split-second of surprise in it for Cardinalli and Pappas, even if they were expecting it. I needed several moments to realize that the show was over and that I needed distance between me and the blast.

We were blocks away in the rain before I looked at Butcher's gray face. I had a tight grin for him. "Like I said, Butcher, there aren't any free tickets to these parties. A double-cross buys you a quick way of dying."

Butcher said nothing. He looked sick. He had a few things to think about. I left it like that. The knife had cut any ties we'd had in a way which wouldn't patch up.

All there was left was to put Butcher on a bench next to a phone booth and call Thierney to tell him where to pick Butcher up. When I hung up, I walked over and stared at Butcher's face for a long time before he looked up at me. There wasn't anything to say. He finally wagged his head and dropped his gaze. I figured it was enough and let it alone.

My damp suit felt as clammy and heavy as a wet stone as I got in the car. The chill that had settled inside me wasn't from the weather. It was a coldness which grew as I drove away. I watched Butcher's figure fall away behind me until he was a huddled form on the bench, with the street lights making a dimmed circle of yellow around him.

The silence with me in the car was the sort that could be as loud as bagpipes in your ears, and my nerves were vibrating like snapped string. I knew that the money in my pocket would buy enough booze to shut the feeling off as usual and put the job in a place I wouldn't remember. The hiss of tires kept me company out of the city. The weather did nothing to dim my urge to leave Chicago.

You don't want to, but you wonder about the bad jobs, the jobs that finish like a game where everyone ran like hell but nobody moved. You wonder because you go away from a job like that with a feeling that something is following you close and that maybe all the losers haven't been counted yet.

It helps to know the ways to buy blank hours. But after the booze and the hookers, you still have an idea that somewhere on the job you took out a loan on time to go on living and you don't know the collection date.